— THE — — END? —

R. J. SLOANE

authorHOUSE®

AuthorHouse™
1663 Liberty Drive
Bloomington, IN 47403
www.authorhouse.com
Phone: 1 (800) 839-8640

© 2019 R. J. Sloane. All rights reserved.

No part of this book may be reproduced, stored in
a retrieval system, or transmitted by any means
without the written permission of the author.

Published by AuthorHouse 10/07/2019

ISBN: 978-1-7283-3039-6 (sc)
ISBN: 978-1-7283-3038-9 (e)

Print information available on the last page.

Any people depicted in stock imagery provided by Getty
Images are models,
and such images are being used for
illustrative purposes only.
Certain stock imagery © Getty Images.

This book is printed on acid-free paper.

Because of the dynamic nature of the Internet, any
web addresses or links contained in this book may
have changed since publication and may no longer
be valid. The views expressed in this work are
solely those of the author and do not necessarily
reflect the views of the publisher, and the publisher
hereby disclaims any responsibility for them.

ACKNOWLEDGEMENTS

My thanks need to go to my two good friends and best critics, Michael Black and Hester Goddard, for their encouragement with this project and for reading an earlier version of this book and suggesting many improvements, most of which I have incorporated here. Thanks should also go to the team at Authorhouse for doing such a splendid job on the presentation of the book and getting it into the marketplace so speedily.

CHAPTER

1

Jenny and David Spiller seemingly had everything: good looks, good jobs, a happy marriage and a lovely house in an affluent suburb of west London. David had inherited this from his parents some ten years earlier after they had both been killed in a car crash. They were the envy of most of their friends, especially as they had no kids to tie them down, and could often be seen out with the 'swinger' set in various bistros and discos in the city. They'd been childhood sweethearts since secondary school, having naturally gravitated together as they were both only children and, back then, had lived near each other. They'd got married straight after university when both of them had found decent jobs in London, a city they both loved, David working in the accounts department of an advertising company in the West End and

Jenny as a research assistant to a Member of Parliament.

However, after many years of relatively unalloyed bliss, except for the usual marital spats and the death of David's parents which had hit him very hard, everything started to fall apart when Jenny decided it was time to start a family. She went off the pill and soon after became pregnant. She and David were now in their late thirties and she knew of course of the danger of having a Down's Syndrome baby when starting a family so late but she refused to have the amniocentesis test done for it, saying that babies had the right to be born, no matter what their condition was. It was a difficult pregnancy and, when she was told after a scan in her 16th week that the baby did indeed have Down's, she just shrugged and refused to have the offered termination. David wasn't so sure if this was a good idea but he knew he couldn't go against her wishes.

So, after a birth which was almost as traumatic as the pregnancy for both David and Jenny, the baby came, a little boy they called Jonathan, and it was then that the trouble really started for David. Jenny refused all offers of help, saying that she could take care of Jonathan by herself, and she stopped working, devoting all her time to him. Their income was cut almost in half overnight, although Jenny did accept the offer of a little financial help from the government, and their lifestyle was forced to change dramatically. They'd known this would happen, of course, but it was still a difficult transition to make.

Long gone were the times when they went out together partying as a couple, going on exotic holidays or having sex whenever one of them wanted it and in came the days when David seemed to spend all his time in the house dealing with tantrums, usually, it's true, by hiding his head in the sand. However, David had to admit that, on the whole, Jonathan was a happy baby and it was almost always Jenny's tantrums he had to deal with. Indeed, on the one occasion when Jenny had had to go up North to visit her parents as her mother was ill, leaving David alone with Jonathan for the first and only time, he'd actually found the time quite relaxing.

But Jenny loved Jonathan - of that there was no doubt in anybody's mind – indeed, doted on him would not be too strong a phrase, to a point that David found positively unhealthy. She lavished all her attention on the baby and started to ignore her husband completely, just snapping at him whenever she absolutely had to speak to him. He just seemed to be an unavoidable irritant, like an old, uncomfortable piece of furniture. Fortunately David still had his own job to go to where he could escape from the pressure cooker atmosphere at home but this was not enough for him. Strangely, deep down he still loved his wife and he adored Jonathan, he knew that, but the sheer amount of time and energy his wife spent on their son meant that she had none left over for him. So, for example, she refused to *ever* get a babysitter in so that just the two of them could go out together for an evening. She said she wouldn't be able to relax with a stranger in the house but would always be worried about Jonathan and they couldn't afford one anyway, which simply wasn't true.

In addition to all this, her libido seemed to have disappeared since her pregnancy and sex with her husband was now something of the past. This disturbed David and he wondered if it was normal. He tried talking to Jenny about it but she refused to discuss it, saying always that she was just too tired to 'do it'. He asked her if she thought a therapist might be a useful option but again she refused to countenance the idea without giving any logical reason for her refusal, except to say that she hated the idea of any form of psychiatry if it applied to her. She was perfectly all right, thank you very much! She certainly wasn't mad!

But a bigger problem than the lack of sex was their now almost complete lack of communication. The times when they could just sit on the sofa relaxing together and chatting about their days or whatever came into their heads were long gone. Now, whenever David returned from work, it was just to a litany of complaints about how tired she was and how she had nobody to help her in the house. David pointed out that Social Services was always there to help if she felt it was necessary but, when this provoked a screaming fit with her shouting at him that she didn't want anybody else near Jonathan, he never raised that option again. He asked her once what she talked about with the social worker who came to the house fairly regularly to check on Jonathan and she admitted she didn't talk to her but just let her in to see Jonathan for a couple of minutes at a time to check on his health. It became as if he were a lodger in his own house and he and his wife were just two ships that passed in the night.

So the atmosphere at home was not a happy one. Their old friends had all drifted away, mainly because Jenny did not make them feel welcome in the house, and, indeed, Jenny herself did not seem to feel the lack of them. David suspected that it had a lot to do with Jonathan's condition, believing Jenny was embarrassed about it.

There were only two people she seemingly talked to about everything on the phone, her parents, and she spent hours doing so but this provoked even more resentment in David who'd always felt they regarded him as a failure and not a suitable partner for their beloved Jenny. Fortunately maybe for him, they lived in Scarborough way up in the north of England so Jenny and David didn't see much of them, although he had to admit they were very good with Jonathan when they did come for one of their rare visits even if they did spoil him rotten.

David could see with alarm the physical consequences of the stress of looking after Jonathan on his wife. She stopped looking after her appearance and was becoming gaunt and haggard, looking more like an old woman than the young, vibrant, beautiful one he'd married. He reckoned she wasn't eating properly and this was yet another cause for concern, but she refused to see the doctor, saying she didn't have time, a ridiculous excuse in his opinion, and anyway didn't need to. She really needed some professional help, he knew, but how could he get her to accept even the idea of it?

However hard he tried, he couldn't get inside Jenny's head and really understand what was going on in there and this worried him almost as much as everything else that was going on. If only she'd sit down and really talk to him, even for two minutes a day! And why, oh, why did everything he said or did make her so angry, so critical? He'd tried everything he could think of to make her happy, hadn't he? He didn't think it had anything to do with post-natal depression but what did he know? He did know, of course, that women could be irrational at times but the situation, in his mind, was becoming intolerable. She was even becoming reluctant now to let *him* near Jonathan. Something would have to change.

CHAPTER 2

'Jenny's' response

I was trawling through 'David's' computer the other day, looking for some old pictures of 'Jonathan', which we only keep on his desktop, and discovered the preceding words of my husband's lurking openly in the directory. He always was hopeless at hiding things from me. So I decided to write the following rebuttal of his points. Oh, yes, I know he's changed all the names and a lot of the details, which is why I've put the names in quotation marks, but he is so clearly writing about us that I simply couldn't let him get away with it. I mean, I can understand his wish for anonymity but who's he trying to kid? I will hide this much more securely than he did so he will never find it. Why am I writing this even if it never sees the light of day? Simply to put my side of the story

THE END?

and to make myself feel a bit better, a kind of catharsis if you like. Is that logical enough or does it sound ridiculous? Well, I don't care either way.

If truth be told, I never knew that 'David' was much of a writer and was actually quite impressed with his persuasiveness. Is the foregoing supposed to be the beginning of something much longer? I will have to keep an eye on it. I certainly don't care if my own writing standard doesn't come up to his. But why the devil does he write in the third person, not the first?? It seems like a weaselly way out.

So his first, and apparently most important, point: His desire to get inside my head to find out what's going on in there.

To be honest, I don't really know myself what's going on in my head. Introspection never was my strong point. All I do know is that I'm acting entirely on my maternal instincts. They are telling me that 'Jonathan' is, by far, the most important thing in my universe at present and I will fight like a tigress to defend his quality of life. If this means spending nearly 24 hours a day with him, so be it. And if that means I don't look after myself as well as I should and get very tired taking care of him, again so be it. I literally don't have the time or energy to spend my evenings chatting with 'David'. And if he can't see that, well, it's just too bad!

Point number 2: The 'embarrassment' factor caused by 'Jonathan'.

This is interesting. I suppose there might be some truth in it. I've never really thought about it, to be honest. But I don't think that's why we no longer have so-called friends. I think it's more that they were only acquaintances in the first place and dropped out of our social circle when they saw 'Jonathan's' condition. *They* were the ones to be embarrassed, not me.

Point number 3: The lack of sex.

I suppose, as a man, he finds it much harder to do without this than a woman. But the fact of the matter is, and he was quite right here, that, since before the baby's birth, I have gone off the whole idea of sex and now, fortunately, we live in an age where he can't force me to do it. It's as simple as that. As for seeing a therapist about it, no way. I know exactly what he/she would say: 'You need to spice up your sex lives. Go out and buy these toys to help you' - and here we'd be presented with a list of them. That really doesn't appeal to me. Whether my sex drive (or 'libido' as my husband so clinically puts it) ever comes back is anybody's guess. I suppose a part of me hopes so but I have no intention of forcing the issue.

Point number 4: My closeness to my parents.

I'm sorry if my husband feels the way he does but there's nothing I can do about it. My parents have always been there for me and I'm certainly not about to change the habits of a lifetime just for him. If he feels isolated because of this, he'll just have to deal with it.

Point number 5: My so-called tantrums.

If I get angry with him, it's always for a good reason. Usually, it's because he's making what I regard as unreasonable demands on me e.g. continually asking me when we might 'do it'. One of his most annoying expressions is "By the way", which I know almost always prefaces some sort of extra demand on my time. He's not a bad man, I know that, and I have to admit that he's good with the baby when he's around but he simply doesn't know what to do if there's any sort of crisis, which, inevitably, there quite often is, and always leaves it up to me to sort out.

Point number 6: Why we never go out alone together any more.

Yes, he's absolutely right when he says that I'm very reluctant to let anyone else near the baby. I'm the only one who knows how to handle him and, if anything happened while we were out, I'd never forgive myself.

I hope that the points I've made here clear up to some degree at least my feelings about my husband's problems with me. I felt it was necessary to rebut his accusations and if, after my death for example, he gets to read this, I hope he will appreciate my point of view a bit better. And, if all this seems very defensive, so what??

CHAPTER 3

But what could David do to change things? He thought about having an affair – he was still relatively young after all and had kept his looks - but then decided it was all too much hassle and anyway he couldn't betray Jenny like that even if it would solve the problem of his sexual frustration. He also thought about maybe threatening to move out but he was too scared that Jenny would just say, 'OK. Go!' He seemed to be a useless appendage in the house and he reckoned that this was a very real possibility. And, anyway, he had nowhere he could easily move to. He had got to the point when he really dreaded going home after work and had taken to doing a lot of overtime so he wouldn't have to.

But finally he decided, when Jonathan was nearly two and a half, that he would speak to his own GP about his and his family's problems and see what she could suggest although even this, in itself, felt like a betrayal of Jenny as he was doing it without her knowledge – behind her back, as it were. So one Monday he rang up his surgery from work and made an appointment to go in and see her that Friday. He would have to take the morning off work, something he very rarely did, but he thought it might be worth it.

When Friday came, he went along to the surgery armed with the notes he'd made in secret at work of what he saw as the family's problems and, after having waited what seemed like hours, finally got in to see the GP. She, he knew from some past experience of her, was a very sympathetic woman, a bit older than him, who would listen to what he had to say and, hopefully, give some wise counsel although he still felt bad about talking to her about such personal stuff.

'It's not a physical problem this time, Doctor, but rather a mental and family one,' he began by saying.

'I'm listening,' she said.

THE END?

So, glancing at his notes from time to time, he poured out all his grievances about Jenny and his worries about her and her apparent obsession with their baby. When he'd finished, he was almost in tears but managed to control himself enough to say, 'I don't know what to do, Doctor. I'm at my wits' end.'

'Well, first,' she replied slowly, 'I'm glad you had the courage to come and see me. I know how difficult it must have been for you.' He managed to smile wanly at her words but then she continued, 'You are not the first person to have developed such problems in your relationship, you know. The birth of a child can be a very traumatic time for both parents, especially the mother, and you both, of course, have had to deal with exceptionally difficult circumstances because of Jonathan's physical condition.' There she paused but soon went on, 'But I know you're not here for general platitudes but for some practical advice,' and he nodded eagerly. 'Do you think she might accept the idea of another mother with a Downs baby coming to see her? I know there are support groups all over the place for parents of children with Downs although I'm not sure where the nearest one would be.'

He perked up when he heard this and said, 'Yes, maybe. And it might just take her out of herself for a bit. I can certainly ask her.'

'Good. And perhaps you could also do some research to find the nearest group to you? Or wait, I may be able to do that right now.' And she started typing away on the computer in front of her. 'Here we go,' she said, turning the computer screen towards him. And there was a list of local organisations which might be able to help! However, none of them specifically mentioned Downs so she narrowed her search and came up with one lady with a contact e-mail address who apparently lived not far away.

'Want to just talk?' the lady's website said. 'I live in West London and have a Downs baby and would love to meet somebody locally who does too. Do send me an e-mail.' It had been posted just a couple of months before.

'There,' the doctor said now. 'She seems to be perfect. Don't you agree?'

'Yes, absolutely!' David replied excitedly, copying down the lady's name and e-mail address. 'I never thought of that idea but, if it works, it might be just the ticket.'

THE END?

'Let me know how you get on,' the doctor said finally and David promised he would.

When he left her office, he glanced at his watch and realised he'd been in there for about forty minutes, far longer than the stipulated ten minutes allocated for each appointment, and thought that he should have thanked her for giving up so much of her precious time for him. But there'd be plenty of time later to make up for it if her idea worked.

CHAPTER 4

David went in to work straight after his appointment with the doctor but found it more difficult than usual to concentrate. He could only think about how he would phrase the doctor's suggestion to Jenny that evening. He decided he wouldn't mention the doctor's involvement at all but merely say it was an idea he'd had at work and would she like to give it a go?

So it was with some trepidation that he opened his front door that evening and went into the house. Everything was quiet and he presumed that Jenny must be putting Jonathan to bed. He crept into Jonathan's bedroom and looked at his son just settling down to sleep. His baby son at once opened his eyes and said 'Dada', one of the few words he had in his vocabulary so far, stretching out his arms to be given a cuddle, which David willingly did. Then he tried to kiss his wife on the cheek but, as usual these days, she just turned her head away and said, 'Can you go now? As you can see, I'm trying to get him down.' So David, defeated, left the child's bedroom and went down to the kitchen where he poured himself a glass of wine and waited for Jenny to join him.

When she did so, she at once started to complain to him about his conduct in coming into Jonathan's bedroom and waking him up. But, as usual, David just let the complaint wash over him, feeling more and more gloomy about the chances of achieving his aim and getting Jenny to contact the lady with the website. But he knew he had to grasp the bull by the horns so when Jenny paused for breath at one point, he said, 'I had an idea today.'

'Oh, what's that, then?' Jenny responded in her usual derisory fashion whenever David suggested something new.

But, at least, she was now listening to him. So he plunged on, 'I was wondering how you'd feel about meeting another mother with a baby like Jonathan?'

'There's no other baby like Jonathan!' Jenny responded angrily.

'No, I know that but you know what I mean.'

'Have you met this mythical creature then?' Jenny said now, her voice dripping with sarcasm.

'No, but I did get an e-mail address off the web,' David responded wearily.

'Clever old you.'

And at this point David almost gave up, thinking, 'It's no use.' But he ploughed manfully on, saying, 'Can I at least show you her website?'

'Yes, I suppose so, if you have to.'

So he took out his smart phone and showed her what he'd last seen in the doctor's office that morning. 'She sounds nice, don't you think?' he said.

'She sounds OK, I suppose,' Jenny said dubiously. 'But you know what I feel about meeting people off the internet. It could be anybody.'

'Yes, I agree but an e-mail wouldn't hurt, would it?'

'No, I suppose not.'

'Why don't you do it now?' he asked, almost pleadingly.

'Yes, all right. But then you'll have to stop bugging me, OK?'

'Yes. Fine,' David said.

So she went into his study, turned on his computer and sent the lady an e-mail, just saying that she too had a baby with Downs and wouldn't mind a brief chat. David was watching her do this like a hawk as he wouldn't have put it past her to have pretended to send the message. 'There, done,' she said. 'Are you happy now?'

'Yes, thanks. Now I guess you'll just have to wait and see if she responds.'

'I rather doubt she will,' Jenny said negatively as she went back into the kitchen and started preparing their supper which, as usual, they ate in silence.

CHAPTER 5

But the lady did respond! The very next evening, when David got home, he found Jenny typing furiously on his computer with Jonathan playing happily with his blocks on his own on the floor.

'What's going on?' he asked.

'That lady, Jane, who you forced me to contact, got back to me and we've been corresponding.'

'That's great!' David said enthusiastically.

'She's even sent me a few photos of her little girl, Emma, and I was just going to send her some of Jonathan when you barged in.'

'OK. I'll leave you to it, then,' David said, feeling happier than he'd been for months.

THE END?

However, supper that evening was its usual silent affair with Jenny not telling him anything further about Jane or Emma, in spite of him tentatively asking, and he finally went up to bed, feeling that perhaps the whole thing had been a waste of time. But the next evening when he got home, he found Jenny happier than she'd been for ages and full of news.

'Jane came over today with Emma and we took the children to the park,' she said.

David knew how difficult Jenny had been finding it to even leave the house and he was delighted to hear this. 'Really?' he said, almost disbelievingly.

'Yes, and we talked for ages.'

'What about?' David asked now.

'Oh, just woman's stuff,' Jenny replied, not going into any detail.

'Is she married?'

'No, divorced. Her husband left her when Emma came along.'

'Because she had Down's?'

'I don't know. We didn't talk about our husbands much.'

'How does she make ends meet?' David asked.

'She designs her own jewellery in her house and sells it to market traders.'

'That sounds rather enterprising.'

'Yes, that was exactly what I said. But she admitted it was very hard to keep it up what with having to look after Emma as well. She was wearing some of it and I loved it. I asked her if she could make me something.'

David was really taken aback by this last statement as he hadn't seen Jenny wearing jewellery or make up since before Jonathan was born. 'So do you think you have made a friend?' he asked tentatively.

'I hope so,' Jenny replied and there the conversation ended, the longest they'd had for months.

A few days after this David came home early one day as he'd been feeling rather poorly at work and found the house empty. He presumed Jenny had just popped out to the local shop with Jonathan. Although she *could* drive if she wanted to and David always left the car for her at home, preferring to walk to the local underground station, she hadn't done so, as far as he was aware, for more than a year. He decided to go upstairs and have a nap, in the hope that this would make him feel better. He fell asleep quickly and was woken by the sound of voices and children squealing down in the kitchen. Surprised, he got up and blearily staggered downstairs.

There he was confronted by a strange sight. Jonathan was playing on the floor with a little girl, who obviously also had Downs, while Jenny was talking animatedly to a lady in a flowery print dress with masses of long brown hair who looked about her age. She was wearing brightly coloured bangles on her wrists and resembled an exotic bird, perhaps a parrot or a bird of paradise. They stopped talking as soon as he came in and Jenny said, accusingly, 'Why on earth are you home so early?' without bothering to introduce him to the lady.

'I didn't feel very well and decided to leave work early. I was upstairs having a nap,' David replied defensively. Then he added, 'Aren't you going to introduce me then?'

'Oh, sorry. Jane, this is my husband, David. David, this is Jane.'

By now David's brain had clicked into gear and he realised it was the lady who he'd got Jenny to e-mail. 'How do you do?' he said politely, shaking her hand. Then he squatted down to the children's level and said to the little girl, 'And you must be Emma?'

She looked up at him and replied proudly and quite distinctly, 'Yes, that's me.' Jonathan still hadn't even registered his presence so David just ruffled his hair and said, 'And how are you, little man?' but Jonathan just shrugged him away, holding up another block to show Emma. 'Well, Emma seems to have made a big hit with Jonathan,' David said, standing up and addressing the two women.

'Yes,' Jane replied. 'They seem to get along quite well.' But then she looked at her watch and said, 'Well, Jenny. I must be off now. Thanks for the company. We must do it again soon.' And she bent down and picked up Emma in one practised swoop and left with her howling in protest.

Then Jonathan started to cry too and Jenny said when they were alone, 'Why do you always have to spoil everything?' which David reckoned was one of the most unfair things anybody had ever said to him. But he didn't respond, knowing that to do so would simply provoke another of Jenny's tantrums.

After Jenny had taken Jonathan upstairs to calm him down and change him and had returned with him, David ventured to say, 'I'm glad both you and Jonathan seem to have made a friend,' but this didn't elicit any response at all so David gave up and went into his study to do some work.

CHAPTER 6

But at least Jenny seemed happier now and was starting to take more care with her appearance, even putting on a little make-up and, occasionally, wearing jewellery. But when David remarked on this change, Jenny said nothing so he dropped the subject.

His doctor phoned him at home one evening after Jenny had gone to bed, purportedly to give him the results of some blood tests he'd needed but really to find out how he was getting on emotionally. He told her about how Jenny had met up with the lady on the internet and how it seemed to have improved her mood a bit although she was still very cold and distant with him. The doctor offered him anti-depressants if he felt he needed them but he declined the offer, not wanting to go down that route unless it became absolutely unavoidable. Anyway, he finished by telling her truthfully, he was more upbeat about the future now. She seemed happy for him and, before he rang off, he thanked her for devoting so much time at the surgery to his problems but she just laughed and said, 'It's all in a day's work.'

Jenny never told him about any future meetings with Jane, which disappointed him as he would have liked to meet her again. He suggested inviting her over to dinner but this was met with a cold, 'No way'. When he asked, reasonably he thought, why not, Jenny said, 'Because Jane is like work for me and I don't mix work and play.' He wanted to pursue this further but didn't dare for fear of provoking another outburst of anger.

But then the situation resolved itself in his favour. Jane rang him late one evening while he was working after Jenny had gone to bed. He explained this to her and she apologised for disturbing him and asked if he could ask his wife whether they could meet up the following day as she unexpectedly had a free day.

'Sure. No problem,' he said but then realised he was desperate to keep her talking. 'Actually, I wanted to thank you for helping

Jenny. As you may have gathered, she's been going through something of a crisis since Jonathan was born.'

'I can understand that. It hasn't exactly been easy for me with Emma, especially with not having anyone to support me.'

'I'm not sure how much support I am for Jenny,' David remarked despondently.

Jane must have picked up on his tone for she said, 'You must be a rock of support for her, surely?'

'Do you think we could meet for lunch one day without the children or Jenny around? I feel I really would like to talk to you further about Jenny,' David said, emboldened by her last remark. There was a long pause at the other end but Jane finally said, 'Yes, I suppose that would be OK.' So they arranged to meet the following Thursday, three days away, at a local bistro for a light lunch. It meant taking a bit of time off work but David knew his boss wouldn't mind. He was owed quite a bit of holiday time, after all. And if he could just get a little more insight into his wife, he knew it would be worth it.

∼

When Thursday came, David dressed and shaved more carefully than usual. He wasn't quite sure why he did this but he felt he ought to try to make a good impression on Jane. They met on schedule at the bistro and were seated at David's request at an out-of-the-way table. After they'd ordered, Jane sat back and said, 'So tell me what's on your mind, David.'

He started hesitantly, trying to explain why he was worried about Jenny, but Jane listened so sympathetically he began to talk about himself and his needs too but without mentioning his sexual frustration. As he was speaking, he was watching Jane carefully for how she would react. But she didn't comment, just listened. He was interrupted when the food came but resumed after they'd eaten. When he'd finally run out of words, he said, 'I'm so sorry to have burdened you with all this but I felt that you, as an outsider, might be able to give me some insight into Jenny. The problem is that I never know what's going on inside her head.'

But Jane just put her hand on David's and said, 'Poor you.' Then she paused with her hand still on David's before continuing, 'I know Jenny's having a hard time coming to terms with Jonathan's condition and I've been trying to help her see a way through the problems but I'm afraid there's only so much I can do. She really needs to take control of the situation by herself. But she's still very fragile.'

'But one of the main problems is that she refuses to see a therapist or even go to the GP for help,' David almost wailed. He didn't take his hand away, however, thinking in some deep part of his brain that it was nice to feel the touch of a woman again. But then he suddenly realised that Jane was, in fact, a very attractive woman in her own right and this shocked him finally into removing his hand from hers. But Jane determinedly picked it up again from the table and held it firmly and this time he didn't resist. He couldn't have even if he'd wanted to.

'But she did get in touch with me,' Jane pointed out.

'Only because I made her,' David replied bitterly.

THE END?

'Oh, really? She didn't tell me that.'

And David went on to recount his visit to the doctor and how she was the one who'd had the idea of looking for somebody in a similar situation, how she'd found Jane's website and how David had given it to Jenny and how reluctant she'd been at first to access it. 'But I invited you here primarily because I wanted to thank you for befriending Jenny, not to talk about myself. She is, at least, certainly looking a bit better than she was.'

'She certainly needs to get out more,' Jane replied. 'Does she drive?'

'Yes,' David said, 'but, as far as I know, she hasn't done so for ages.'

'I will try and get her to come over to my place with Jonathan.'

'Would you? That would be a real breakthrough!' David exclaimed.

'In the meantime would you like to come back with me for coffee? I have to get home soon to deal with Emma. I don't like to leave her for too long with the babysitter.'

David looked at his watch and realised that it was already halfway through the afternoon and too late to return to work. 'Sorry,' he said. 'I didn't realise it was so late. I really have been blathering on, haven't I? But yes, I'd love that if you're sure.'

Jane laughed and said, 'I wouldn't have invited you if I wasn't sure.' And David realised she thought she was quite safe with him. He hoped she was.

They took a taxi back to Jane's place which turned out to be a pretty little maisonette in a quiet suburban street lined with trees. She opened the front door and they went in, meeting the babysitter who was just putting on her coat.

'Did you see us arriving, Lucy?' Jane asked the young brunette.

'Yes, I was watching out for you. Emma's fine. She's watching TV.' While she was talking, Lucy was eyeing up David and when she left, he saw her roll her eyes at Jane. But Jane simply ignored her, saying just, 'Thanks, Lucy. See you soon.'

When they were alone, except for Emma who was watching a noisy cartoon in the living room, Jane took David into the kitchen which was quite large and started to make coffee. 'Emma will be fine for hours now. She could watch cartoons quite happily all day if I let her.'

'We've tried getting Jonathan to watch cartoons on the TV but he loses concentration so quickly and gets distracted.'

'You've got to keep at it. Emma was like that for ages but now TV's the best pacifier I could wish for.'

'How old is she?'

'Three and a half now. I just take one day at a time and hope for the best for her.'

'I wish Jenny had an outlook like yours. Tell me, Jane. Do you miss having a man around?'

'It depends on the man. If you're asking about my ex, no, not at all. He was totally useless.'

'That's exactly what I'm always accused of being by Jenny.'

'That's us women for you, I'm afraid. We're never satisfied.' Jane put David's coffee in front of him and sat next to him at the breakfast counter. She reached for his hand again and studied the lines on it.

'Are you a palm reader?' David asked.

'I've meddled in it a bit,' Jane said.

'And what do you see?'

'You are going to meet a tall, dark, handsome stranger, fall in love, get married and have lots of babies.'

David almost fell off the stool he was laughing so much. 'I bet that's what you say to all the guys.'

'No, not necessarily. Sometimes I tell the truth.'

She was very close to him now and he could smell her hair. It smelled like cinnamon and chocolate. Suddenly he was possessed by an overwhelming urge to take her in his arms and kiss her until she melted. But all he did was to bend his head and kiss the back of her hand lightly. She responded by turning to face him and looking directly into his eyes. 'Do you like me, David?'

'Yes, I do. Perhaps too much,' he replied ruefully.

Then she leaned forward and kissed him on the lips. A bolt of pure electricity went through him and he grasped her by the waist and pulled her towards him. He found himself kissing her passionately and she was responding, much to his surprise. The next thing he knew was them both tearing their clothes off and making love on the cold, hard kitchen floor. It was probably the most passionate bout of love making he'd ever experienced and he didn't want it ever to stop. In the end it did stop but only when he started pleading for mercy and both their bodies were shiny with sweat. She got off him finally and nonchalantly started dressing but watching him openly all the while. He wondered then where it was going to lead, this awful mistake on his part, but she put him at his ease somewhat by saying, 'Now, David, please don't start feeling guilty. You wanted it as much as I did, didn't you?' and he had to admit it. 'And, by the way, I'm not a nymphomaniac. Just a rather lonely woman who needs a man occasionally.'

'So I was doing you a service, was I?' he asked.

'Yes, if you want to look at it like that.'

'Oh, good. That's OK, then,' he said rather bitterly.

But she knelt down beside him and, taking his by now flaccid penis in her hand, started to stimulate him again. And, as before, he found he couldn't resist her. They made love once more but this time much more tenderly and she made him feel like a million dollars.

'Can I see you again?' he asked shyly when he was fully dressed again.

'Are you sure you want to?'

'Yes, absolutely one hundred per cent sure.'

'Well, in that case, I don't see why not.'

'I'll give you a ring,' he said as he was leaving.

'Do that,' she replied. And there they left it.

David went home in a taxi but asked to be dropped off at the underground station as he

THE END?

wanted to walk home like he always did. He certainly didn't want to be spotted by Jenny rolling up to the front door in a taxi. If she spotted it, that would arouse her suspicions for sure. He was mulling over what had happened the entire way, replaying every word and scene in his mind over and over again. Had he been seduced? He rather thought he had but he couldn't give a toss. He knew he'd enjoyed it. He was feeling better about himself than he'd felt since before Jonathan's birth. But at the same time he knew he felt guilty about betraying Jenny but not too guilty. If only she'd shown him a little more appreciation over the past couple of years, he'd never had gone near Jane. It was a strange mixture of emotions.

He looked at his watch as he opened his front door and was relieved to see he'd timed it perfectly. It was almost exactly the time he always came back from work. Jenny was in Jonathan's bedroom putting him to bed so he went straight into the bathroom and had a quick shower, putting all the clothes he'd been wearing in the laundry basket. When he came out, he hoped he didn't still smell of Jane.

But Jenny said nothing to him of any suspicions and he thought he'd got away with it. Their relationship remained very cool, however, and David's place as a real member of the family didn't seem to have improved.

He managed to refrain from calling Jane until the following Tuesday but when he did, she wasn't in and he didn't want to leave a message. He tried again the next day and this time she was there. 'Do you still want to see me?' he asked.

She laughed and said, 'I thought it was *you* who wanted to see *me*.'

'You know I do.'

'Well, OK, then. When can you come over?'

His heart leaped when he heard this and he said rather timidly, 'I was hoping to come this Friday afternoon at about 2.'

'Let me just check my diary. Yes, that looks OK.'

'Great. See you then,' and he hung up.

Friday afternoons were a good time for him to leave the office early as most of the other employees did so too, hoping to escape the rush hour and be home in time to have a decent weekend. He'd already thought of a good excuse to tell Jenny if he happened to be late.

On Friday morning he took good care of his appearance and left the house in a state of high excitement. He tried to kiss Jenny goodbye but she turned her head away and all he got was a mouthful of hair. That made him feel better about what he was going to be doing that afternoon.

CHAPTER 7

'Jenny's' reaction

I've been reading the new 'chapters' of my husband's story avidly but, as they've been purely factual, just detailing what's been going on, except for the stuff about the doctor first instigating my meeting with 'Jane', which I didn't know, I haven't bothered to write anything. However, now, after the last revelatory chapter, I feel I must. And, oh boy, what a revelation it was!

So 'David' is having an affair with 'Jane', my new friend! How do I feel about that? Strangely, I'm neither very surprised nor angry nor indeed jealous. In fact, I feel detached from the whole thing, as if it was happening to somebody else or was in a novel. In fact, I just feel completely numb. This might seem rather an odd reaction. After all, we have been married for nearly twenty years now and I thought I knew my husband well enough to trust him around other women. But the fact is I really couldn't care less. I almost feel 'Good for him!' Does this mean we're now living in what they used to call 'an open marriage'? For my part, however, I have no intention of finding another man or, indeed, giving my husband a divorce if he should happen to ask for one. He's not getting out of his marriage vows that easily although maybe I'll change my mind about that later.

My only real regret is that maybe I've lost my friend. Surely she wouldn't dare have the cheek to see me again after this, would she? And that would be a pity, especially as I was just starting to get used to living in the real world again. Oh well, que sera, sera.

One advantage I can see from this situation is that, hopefully, I won't have my husband under my feet all the time, asking his unreasonable demands of my body. I don't think for a moment, however, that he will leave home. He's too tied to the baby. And another obvious advantage I've just thought of is that, if he ever accuses me to my face of being cold and distant, I can always point out that he *is* sleeping with my friend and how else should I behave?

It will be interesting to see how all this pans out.

CHAPTER 8

Straight after a quick lunch in town that Friday, David took a taxi over to Jane's house and was dropped outside the door. She opened it at once and led him inside. There was no sign of a babysitter this time and the house was quiet.

'Where's Emma?' he asked.

'I just put her down for her afternoon nap. Hopefully she'll sleep for quite a while.' And she led him upstairs this time to her bedroom which was decorated in bright colours, much like he'd imagined. There they got undressed quickly and collapsed onto her bed.

'It's more comfortable than the kitchen floor,' David remarked as he was nibbling her ear and she giggled. But she quickly became serious and soon they were in the throes of lovemaking with her bed creaking as they bounced on it passionately. It was every bit as good as David remembered and he all but forgot Jenny. Jane seemed to enjoy it too, coming again and again, crying out each time she did. And this time he used what little experience of women he had to make sure she enjoyed it, even managing to postpone his own ejaculations at least twice.

Finally, when they were both sated, he rolled over on his side and looked at her directly. 'That was fun, wasn't it?' he said.

'Mmmm,' she agreed, snuggling up next to him. 'How long can you stay?'

He looked at his watch and saw it was still only 3.15. 'Another hour and a half?' he said hopefully.

'Plenty of time then,' she said and started to stroke him gently. But then Emma came in, rubbing sleep out of her eyes, and goggled at the two of them in bed together. Jane immediately jumped out of bed and, putting on a dressing gown, led her downstairs where David soon heard the sound of the TV making its manic cartoon noises. He wasn't sure whether to get up and get dressed but he was so comfortable and warm in Jane's bed he just continued to lie there. He felt bad about Emma seeing him in bed with her mother but figured that Jane could deal with it.

It wasn't long, however, till Jane came back and said, 'Now where were we?' and continued from where she'd left off.

David quickly found himself growing hard again and managed to have two more orgasms. But he finally admitted defeat and said, 'Can we talk?'

'Sure. What about?'

'Am I just a plaything for you?' he asked seriously.

'No, certainly not,' she said indignantly. 'You are much more important to me than that.'

'You know, don't you, that you are important to me too?'

'Yes, I'd kind of guessed that from the urgency with which you make love,' she said, smiling at him.

He grinned back and said, 'Sorry about that.'

'Oh, there's no need to apologise,' she said, still smiling.

'It's just that I haven't done it with Jenny for so long, I was afraid I might have forgotten how to.'

'It's like riding a bike. Once one has learnt, one never forgets.'

'I'm being serious, Jane,' he said now.

'I know you are, darling,' she replied. 'And I guessed the lack of sex was probably most of your problem.'

'If only it were,' he said gloomily.

'Well, you're always welcome in here,' she said patting the bed. 'Would you like to have a shower?'

'Yes, I'd love to,' he said.

'It's just through there,' she said, pointing at another door leading off from the bedroom and getting up. 'I'll be downstairs in the kitchen preparing Emma's tea. Perhaps we could have a glass of wine before you go.'

'Yes, I'd love that too.'

He went into Jane's spacious en suite bathroom and took a long, leisurely shower before dressing and going downstairs. Emma was sitting in the kitchen, drawing at the table, and she looked up when he came in. 'Are you going to be my Daddy?' she asked clearly enough for David to understand her at once.

David was totally nonplussed and had no idea what to say to this question but Jane came to his rescue. 'Don't be silly, darling. David is just a good friend.'

'Oh,' Emma said and went back to her drawing.

Then Jane fed Emma and gave David his promised glass of wine, having one herself. As he was leaving, Jane said, 'Don't worry about Emma. She will have forgotten all about you by the time she goes to bed.' And he was reassured by her words.

On the way home he questioned whether perhaps he was falling in love with Jane.

He knew he was in lust with her, that much was obvious, but that wasn't the same at all. However, he didn't have a clue where it was all going to end up, except that he suspected it would probably all finish in tears. But he'd cross that bridge when he came to it.

CHAPTER 9

The affair continued with David visiting Jane at her house at more and more frequent intervals. He simply couldn't get enough of her and wondered how Jenny hadn't spotted any signs yet of his infidelity. But she was wrapped up in her own little world of Jonathan, outside of which there appeared to be nothing at all. He doubted whether, even if he confessed, she would be interested enough to care, although he certainly wasn't about to do that. He didn't know if Jenny was still seeing Jane and he didn't ask either of them, feeling that it had nothing to do with him.

But then disaster struck from a totally unexpected quarter. Jonathan became seriously ill with liver failure, one of the possible side effects of Down's, and had to be hospitalised. It was touch and go for a while whether he'd survive and Jenny took to sleeping in the hospital with him. He did, however, pull through and David, who had been distraught throughout the whole episode and hadn't seen Jane at all, was so relieved when Jenny rang him with the news that he burst into tears and rushed straight round to the hospital in a taxi. Without thinking, his eyes still blurry from his tears, he gave Jenny a big impulsive hug and she, rather than pushing him away, hugged him back. Could this be a turning point in their relationship? he thought as soon as he stepped away from his wife.

But she refused to talk to him about the episode of the hug and it was never repeated and, when, after a couple of weeks, she finally got home with Jonathan, she quickly reverted to her old silent ways, only speaking to him when she absolutely had to and usually snapping when she did. David asked her if she wanted him to sleep in the spare bedroom so that she could stay with Jonathan in their bed but she said simply, 'I don't care.' So David took to sleeping there and at once felt better, less guilty about Jane, for it.

But then he felt he had no alternative but to return to Jane and resume their old relationship. He realised how much he was starting to rely on Jane for moral support as well as the sex. Without her he knew he would simply fall to pieces and, when they'd got together again and he'd told her this and about Jonathan's illness, she gave him a big cuddle and said, 'You know I'll always be here for you if you need me, David,' and her kind words almost made him cry.

With a sob in his voice, he replied simply, 'Thank you, Jane.'

'Now, now. Let's not get too maudlin, OK?' she said.

'OK,' he replied, strangling the sob.

But then he felt he simply had to ask Jane the question that had been bothering him for ages. 'Are you still seeing Jenny?' he said.

'I kind of assumed you wouldn't want to know,' she replied. 'But for your information, I have seen her a couple of times in the past few weeks. And, before you ask, I agree with you that some professional help would be useful for her but she won't listen to me.'

'She won't listen to me either,' he said bitterly. 'What do you talk about with her?'

'Almost exclusively the children,' she replied.

'Yes, I might have guessed that.'

'The last time I saw her, I asked whether she might like me to come round and babysit one evening while you two went out but she prevaricated, saying just "I'll see". And I've heard nothing further about my suggestion.'

'Well, thank you for trying anyway,' David said. And then he had to leave.

∼

David's life was now gliding along quite smoothly. He supposed he had a mistress of sorts who relieved his sexual frustrations and whom he thought he might love for her kindness to him and her native common sense. In the past he never would have believed he could have loved two women at the same time, although he had read about such things happening, but now his views had changed. He still knew in his core that he loved Jenny but was it more now for Jonathan's sake? He honestly wasn't sure and he had nobody he could talk to about it.

THE END?

His closest old friends, who happened to be exclusively male, were all getting on with their lives. Most of them had moved far away, often abroad, and those that were left were tied down with their own families and would probably be shocked if he told them about his own life and its problems. Now he just had acquaintances, mainly from his work place, with whom it seemed he could only chat about blokey things like football and TV programmes. And he didn't want to unburden himself to his doctor again. So he felt pretty isolated from his old world but knew also he couldn't or shouldn't complain.

Soon, however, summer came round again and it was nearly time for Jonathan's third birthday. He broached the idea tentatively to Jenny about the possibility of having a party for him but this was immediately vetoed on the spurious, to his mind, grounds that Jonathan wouldn't enjoy it and, anyway, who could they invite? Then he remembered that Emma, Jane's daughter, was almost exactly a year older than Jonathan and the next time he saw Jane he asked her if Emma had ever had a birthday party.

She looked at him and said, 'Actually, no. I've never thought it was worth it as she wouldn't understand what's going on.'

'Are you sure?' he said. 'Wouldn't it be nice to have a joint party with Jonathan?'

She considered the idea for a moment and then replied, 'Yes, on second thoughts, I think it might be fun. I'll ask Jenny if she'd like to come round here with you and Jonathan and we'll have just a small do with the five of us. I'll get some games organised if she could bring a cake. I'm not sure, however, how much persuading I'll need to do.'

'Don't you have any friends around here with small kids who might like to come?'

'Yes but I'm pretty sure Jenny wouldn't come if she knew there were going to be other children around plus their parents.'

David could see the logic in this and agreed to let her talk to Jenny about the idea of just having a party for the five of them.

And when he came home from work one day not long after this conversation, he found Jenny wrapping presents for Jonathan and

THE END?

some obviously for a small girl. 'What's going on?' he asked.

'We're going to Jane's for Jonathan's birthday,' she announced. 'She's having a small party just for Emma and him. Did you know that Emma will be four only a couple of days after Jonathan will turn three?'

'No, I didn't', he answered truthfully. 'OK. That sounds like it could be fun.' He didn't mention, needless to say, that it was he who had initiated the idea in the first place. But he was pleased that Jane had managed to persuade his wife. At least, he thought, it will get her out of the house for a while.

∽

The Saturday nearest to both their birthdays came round quickly. David hadn't visited Jane on the Friday like he usually did, thinking that it would be inappropriate if he was going over the following day with his wife. So in the afternoon he drove the three of them over to Jane's place, being careful to ask Jenny for her address and putting it scrupulously into his Satnav in case she got suspicious if he drove straight there.

On their arrival they found the house decorated with lots of balloons and with a big pile of presents in the living room. David was careful to praise Jane for the decor in the house, not wanting Jenny to think he'd ever been there before, before going outside and bringing in all the stuff they'd brought from the car.

Then the party proper started and the children seemed to love tearing open their presents and sharing them. After that it was time for some games in the small back garden which Jane directed with a firm but fair hand, making sure that each of the children had their turn at winning. David noticed his wife looking on with approval and possibly a touch of jealousy. He reckoned that, if she was jealous, it could be put down to the fact that she wasn't cut out to do such things herself.

After that, it was time for tea and Jenny made a big thing out of cutting the cake she'd brought and giving the children exactly the same size slice each. After everybody had eaten and drunk their fill of orange squash, the kids continued playing with their new toys on the kitchen floor when David, who'd been playing with them, suddenly realised he needed a pee. He looked around for the women and saw Jane stacking the dirty plates in the dishwasher. But where was his wife? He couldn't see her and asked Jane where she was.

'I've no idea. But she won't have gone far,' she said.

David was sorely tempted to go up to her and touch her but he didn't dare, knowing that Jenny could come back at any moment. 'I need a pee,' he said. 'Too much orange squash.'

'Well, you know where it is,' Jane whispered.

So David went upstairs and crossed the hall into Jane's bedroom, aiming to go in her en suite bathroom where he always went. But when he entered the room, he was confronted by a sight both amazing and terrifying to him. Jenny was lying on her stomach on Jane's bed with her face buried in the pillow which David always used and sobbing her heart out. He had no idea what to do or say but, after a second's pause, managed to ask, 'Whatever's the matter, darling?' But she didn't reply, just getting up and drying her eyes on a tissue she pulled from her sleeve before stalking out of the room.

David sat on the bed, totally nonplussed, wondering what on earth that was all about. He'd never before seen Jenny cry on her own – oh, she often did at home but it was always the result of some accident or other, usually that had happened to Jonathan, and she always seemed to do it in front of him. He simply couldn't imagine what had provoked the crying fit. She'd seemed quite happy while she was downstairs. He finally gave up speculating and went into the bathroom and urinated.

When he had gone downstairs again, he found Jenny with red-rimmed eyes, busy packing up everything they were taking home. She asked him in a shaky voice if he could deal with Jonathan so he picked him up, wailing now, and took him out to the car, strapping him into his car seat. Then Jenny appeared, laden with all Jonathan's new toys, got into the car herself and demanded to be taken home. David didn't even have time to say goodbye to Jane or thank her for having them. She had come out to see them off and caught his eye, giving a small shrug. David could only roll his eyes at her in exasperation before he found himself driving away.

THE END?

Jenny didn't say a word to him on the way home and the silence continued for the rest of the day. David didn't dare to break it, thinking that his wife would explain in her own good time, but he finally got so annoyed with her that he went down to his local for a swift pint or two, something he very rarely did, and when he got back, Jenny was already in bed with Jonathan. So David crept up to the spare bedroom, where he always now slept, and, after washing, lay down and, not very successfully, tried to sleep.

CHAPTER 10

'Jenny's' explanation

So you want to know what provoked my crying fit, do you 'David'? Well, I'll tell you. I was tired and felt like a lie down so I went upstairs, found 'Jane's' bedroom and lay down for a well-deserved rest. I reckoned she wouldn't mind and you two seemed to be absorbed with playing with the kids. But then, when I turned over, I detected the distinctive smell of your aftershave on the pillowcase and realised all of a sudden just how jealous I was of 'Jane'. I know I said previously that I couldn't have cared less about you having an affair but being confronted by some actual hard evidence was something else. Do you understand now?

THE END?

Anyway, my reason for writing this is not to explain myself but to tell you – in secret – that I've come to a decision. I'm going to take 'Jonathan' away for a bit on the train up to my parents. I'm not going to take much with me except a few things for 'Jonathan' as I have plenty of old clothes up there already. I know they'll understand and give him all the love he needs. I have tried to be a good mother but fear I might have failed. Whether I come back or not is in the lap of the Gods.

So goodbye, 'David' – temporarily, at least.

Oh, and, by the way, you said you were distraught when 'Jonathan' got ill. How do you think *I* felt? Not a word about my feelings!

CHAPTER 11

A few days after the abortive birthday party, David returned from work to find the house completely empty and silent. He assumed that Jenny had perhaps taken Jonathan out somewhere, maybe even back to Jane's, and didn't worry but went into his study to do some work. However, when she hadn't returned by dinner time, he started to get frantic. She was *always* home by now! He rang Jane and asked her whether she'd seen his wife but she said, 'No, not since the party' and he explained his concern to her. 'Wait a bit longer till you do anything drastic like call the police,' she said and then added, 'Did she leave any kind of note?' David admitted he hadn't looked for one but said he would do so immediately. So he hung up and went around the house to see if Jenny had left him anything in the way of a note to explain her sudden absence.

THE END?

And he found it on his bedside table in the spare room. It was terse and to the point and said simply, 'Have taken Jonathan up to my parents for a while. The sea air should do him good and I think we both need some space to figure out where we're going. Please don't ring. I'll get in touch when I'm ready.' That was all! It wasn't even signed but David recognised her handwriting.

He was relieved and angry with her at the same time, relieved that she and Jonathan were safe but angry that she hadn't told him about this sudden plan. Then he started to think of the ramifications of what she'd done. Obviously he'd have to take care of himself for a while, which meant all kinds of tedious things like shopping and ironing his shirts but he knew he could cope with that. But what if she decided to stay away permanently? Where would that leave him? It would mean he'd probably never see Jonathan again for one thing, something he reckoned he probably *couldn't* cope with. But that was a worst-case scenario, wasn't it? Oh, and what did she mean by "where we're going"?

He knew he'd go mad if he tried to speculate any further so instead he called Jane back and told her the contents of the note he'd found and his feelings about it. He needed her common sense and she duly delivered it, saying, 'Well, you know where they are, don't you? Isn't that the most important thing? If the worst comes to the worst, you can always go up there and have it out with her.' He knew she was right and thanked her for the advice but she just shrugged off his thanks saying, 'If you want to thank me, you can jolly well do it in person, not just on the telephone.'

'Is that an invitation to come over?' he asked.

'Of course it is, you big dope, and don't forget to bring your nightie.'

That made him smile for the first time at home since long before he'd read the note and also made him realise that it would be the first time he'd stayed the night with her. 'OK, thanks,' he said. 'I'll just have a quick bite to eat here if I can find anything in the kitchen and I'll be right over.'

'Don't be too long, darling, or I might change my mind.' And on that note the conversation ended.

He quickly packed a few essentials for the night, wondering while he did so if this was the ultimate betrayal of his wife – going to the house of his lover to spend the night straight after his wife had 'left' him – but didn't worry about it. He knew he had to have the warmth of Jane next to him, tonight of all nights. And after a quick bowl of tinned soup, he got the car out and drove over to Jane's.

When he got there, he fell into her arms and burst into tears.

'My poor David,' Jane cooed, cuddling him just like he'd seen her do with Emma after she'd fallen over.

But they didn't waste much time and were soon in bed where David felt safe in her arms. He didn't get much sleep that night but woke up in the morning feeling miles better than he had. He had a quick shower, got dressed, putting on a clean shirt he'd brought with him, had some breakfast, and left to go to work. But he didn't forget to give Jane a passionate kiss on the way out, promising her he'd see her that evening.

CHAPTER 12

The next few days went by tranquilly enough with David returning back home every evening after work, half expecting Jenny and Jonathan to have returned, and, when they hadn't, going over to Jane's to spend the night.

But then on that Friday evening when he got back home, he saw he had a message on his answer phone. He pressed Play and heard the voice of his father-in-law saying, 'David, this is Jim. Please give me a call as soon as you get in. I don't have your work number otherwise I would have called you there.'

He sounded distraught and David wondered what had happened. His father-in-law *never* called him! Had something bad happened to Jonathan? He immediately dialled the number in Scarborough, although he had to

THE END?

look it up in his address book first as he rang them so seldom.

The phone was snatched up almost at once and he heard the voice of his father-in-law again. 'David, is that you?'

'Yes, what's going on? You have me worried. Is everything OK with Jonathan?'

'Yes, everything's fine with him. He's sleeping now. It's Jenny!'

David gave a sigh of relief and then asked, 'Why? What's the matter with her?'

'She left early this morning and hasn't returned! It's not like her at all! I've even called the police but they say they can't do anything until she's been gone for 24 hours! They told me she was an adult and could go where she wanted. She hasn't been herself since she arrived! We sort of gathered that you two had had a row. Is that true?'

David could hear the exclamation marks in Jim's voice and agreed with him that it wasn't like her at all to leave Jonathan alone with anybody, even her parents, for so long. But then he remembered Jane's advice to him after she'd first left. 'Did she leave a note?' he asked, without mentioning the possibility of a row.

'We haven't looked for one,' Jim admitted.

'Well, perhaps you should do so.'

'Yes, that's good advice. I'll have a scout round and get back to you.' And then he abruptly hung up.

David was quite worried himself now but quickly rang Jane to let her know he might be late that evening. Then he just sat by the phone.

When it rang, he grabbed it and heard the broken voice of his father-in-law and the sound of Madeleine, his mother-in-law, crying in the background. 'Yes, we found a note,' he said sombrely. 'She left it on her dresser in her bedroom. I'll read it to you: "Dear Mummy and Daddy. I feel that I've reached the end of the road. My marriage is clearly in a terminal state and I've completely lost confidence in my parenting skills. I know you'll look after Jonathan well, at least until David turns up to claim him. So it's goodbye then and I thank you for everything you've tried to do for me. Jenny." And that's it! You don't think she's....'

and here his voice broke completely and David could hear his tears over the phone.

David was in shock when he heard this and couldn't say anything at first. But, when his voice returned, he blurted out, 'I don't know. She was behaving very strangely before she left. But surely now you have enough evidence to call the police?'

'Yes. That's true. But I wanted you to know before I did that.'

'Thank you. That was kind of you. I'm coming up to Scarborough, of course. I'll get a night train and should be with you by the morning.' David had no regrets about this sudden decision. He knew he *had* to be with his parents-in-law, for them as well as for Jonathan, at this time.

'Thank you, David. We'll see you when you arrive. Turn up any time. I'll ring the police now.'

David said his goodbyes and contemplated what he had to do. First he rang for a taxi, then quickly threw a few clothes into a suitcase and carted it downstairs. He'd almost forgotten about Jane in his hurry to leave but he put his mobile phone in his pocket along with his wallet, checking that his credit card was still inside. The taxi came quite soon and he asked the driver to take him to King's Cross. On the way he phoned to tell Jane what was going on and she was very sympathetic, finishing their short conversation by saying, 'Do what you have to do, David.'

When he got to the station at about 8pm, he found to his relief that the train going up to Scarborough was already waiting. He managed to get a ticket quickly – the station wasn't too busy at that time of the evening – and jumped on board, lugging his suitcase. He spent the entire journey looking out of the window but seeing nothing, contemplating a possible future without Jenny. How did he feel about that? He wasn't at all sure. And what would it mean for himself and Jonathan? Would it / *could it* include Jane? But he knew it was useless to speculate. First he needed some evidence that Jenny had, indeed, done away with herself as her note suggested.

He finally got to Scarborough about 11.30 pm and took a taxi to his parents-in-law's house. He'd completely forgotten to phone them on the train but he figured they'd still be up and he was right. They both came to the door when he rang the bell and Madeleine,

THE END?

Jenny's mother, gave him a tearful hug while Jim shook his hand vigorously. They looked much the worse for wear. Madeleine's hair, which she was normally so proud of, was a mess and Jim hadn't shaved and had food stains on the front of his cardigan. They both smelled of whisky and seemed to have aged massively since he'd last seen them. But David couldn't blame them. If a child of his had gone missing, he would be in an even worse state, he knew.

'Any news?' he asked.

'No. The police said they couldn't do anything until daylight,' Jim replied, slurring his words slightly. 'But at least they promised to initiate a full-scale search if she hasn't turned up by then. A policewoman, called Rose, came round and took away a picture of her and made lots of notes. Jenny doesn't seem to have taken any money with her, by the way.'

'OK,' David said, taking charge, but thinking the worst when he heard Jenny had no money on her. 'Why don't you two go up to bed? I'll man the phone. I'll sleep on the sofa next to it. Can I see Jonathan first though?'

'Thank you, David, but I'm sure we wouldn't be able to sleep,' Madeleine said. 'But yes, of course you can see Jonathan.' She led him up the stairs and into the small back bedroom which David immediately saw had been kitted out as a nursery. His son was lying in a large cot with a nightlight on next to him, fast asleep and snoring softly. David went up to him and kissed him gently on the cheek before leaving the room and closing the door quietly. As they were going back downstairs, Madeleine asked, 'Have you had anything to eat?' and David, who hadn't eaten since lunchtime, felt his stomach grumble at the mention of food.

'Well, actually, no,' he admitted. 'In all the rush, I just forgot.'

'Come into the kitchen and I'll make you a sandwich or something.'

So, giving up on taking charge, he followed her into their big, modern kitchen where Madeleine gave him some homemade soup and a sandwich. He felt better afterwards and thanked her.

'No, thank *you* for coming all the way up here so quickly,' she said. 'However,' she added, 'I think I might be able to sleep a bit now you're here so, if I can drag Jim away from the whisky bottle, we'll both go up to bed.'

'Do that,' David said and she left.

CHAPTER 13

The next morning David, who had indeed slept but badly on the sofa, was woken by the sound of Jonathan bawling his head off and, after his brain had started working and he'd remembered where he was, he realised that it was probably the first time in his life his son hadn't had his mother there when he woke up. He got up and staggered upstairs where he found Jonathan in the middle of a full-blown tantrum with Madeleine trying to comfort him, still in her nightie. However, when Jonathan saw his father, he immediately gave an excited squeal and stopped crying. David went up to him and picked him up, giving him a big cuddle. His son snuggled into his arms and quickly went back to sleep again while Madeleine looked on approvingly. David put him down in his cot and then turned to Madeleine.

'What time is it?' he whispered so as not to wake Jonathan.

'About 7, I think,' she replied, also in a whisper.

David did a quick calculation and reckoned he'd managed less than six hours sleep. But it was enough. He felt reasonably awake now and knew he could keep going for as long as was necessary. He peered through the curtains of Jonathan's bedroom and saw it was a fine day with the sun already up.

'Come on down to the kitchen,' Madeleine said, 'and I'll make you some breakfast. It's probably going to be a long day. Jim's still in bed and I think we should let him sleep.'

'Thanks, Madeleine. Can I have a quick shower first?'

'Of course. You remember where the bathroom is?'

And so the day started normally enough although David was surprised by how calm his mother-in-law seemed to be. But then all women were unfathomable to him.

After breakfast David asked Madeleine if he could have the local police's phone number. She gave it to him and he keyed it into his own phone. He dialled, explained who he was and very quickly got through to the same policewoman, Rose, who'd come round to visit his parents-in-law the evening before.

She said, 'I'm going to be your liaison officer in this case. I understand your Jenny's husband.'

'Yes, that's right. Is there any news of my wife?' he asked.

'Where are you?' she asked now without answering his question.

'I'm at my parents-in-law's house in Scarborough. I came up from London last night.'

'Good. I'm glad you're here. No, we have no news yet but we're taking the disappearance of your wife very seriously, especially in view of your son's condition.'

'So what are you actually doing?' David asked, almost angrily.

THE END?

'We've sent your wife's picture and description to all the local forces and instituted a search of the coastal paths around the area as well as putting the coastguard on lookout. We will ring you at once if there's any news.'

'Is there anything I can do to help?'

'No, not really. Not at the moment. Best to leave it to the professionals.'

'Would it be OK if I did my own search in the vicinity? I don't think I can stay cooped up in the house while others are out looking for her.'

She hesitated a moment and then said, 'I don't suppose it could do any harm.'

'OK. I'm going out now then. My parents-in-law will be here to answer the phone.'

'Fine. I'll come round to see you later. Could you be back by around 11?'

'Yes, of course.' And there the conversation ended.

David went off to find Madeleine and tell her that he was going out for a while and when he should be back. He found her in the bathroom putting on her make-up, with her hair all nicely combed as he was used to seeing her. Then he put on a stout pair of walking shoes he'd brought with him and left the house. There was still no sign of Jim.

He knew most of the coastal paths nearby as he had walked along them in his younger days with Jenny after his parents-in-law had moved up from London. So, setting off, he just started walking with no fixed destination in mind and quickly came across small groups of policemen combing the area. He didn't disturb them but carried on walking. He assumed they thought he was just another rambler out in the sunshine.

Quite soon he came to some steep cliffs and, being careful not to fall, peered over the edge to see if he could spot Jenny below. He reckoned that, if *he* was going to top himself, this would be an ideal place to do it. But he couldn't see anything except the waves crashing against the foot of the cliff and when he looked out to sea, saw no signs of a coast guard vessel either. So, finally, looking at his watch and realising time was getting on, he reluctantly turned round and trudged wearily back.

THE END?

He came into the house to find Jim up and about in the kitchen with a large mug of coffee in front of him, as neatly turned out as ever, but with a hangdog expression on his face. David could find no words, however, to cheer him up with. So he just asked 'Any news?'

'No, none,' Jim replied shortly.

'Where's Jonathan?' David asked now.

'Upstairs, playing with Maddie.'

'I suppose I'd better go and relieve her,' David said but this elicited no response at all so he went upstairs to find his son playing happily with his favourite wooden blocks. Madeleine was sitting on a chair watching him. He looked at her closely and thought that, in spite of her neat turn-out, she was actually aging before his eyes. But he said nothing of this to her, just, 'I'll take over sentry duty now. You go and have a rest,' at which she smiled wanly and left the room without a word. He played with Jonathan for a bit but then heard the front door bell go and, scooping up his son, ran downstairs with him.

CHAPTER 14

It was Rose, the policewoman he'd spoken to earlier on the phone. 'We have no news yet but I'd like to speak to you in private if I may,' she said after he'd introduced himself. So, handing Jonathan over to Madeleine who was standing next to him in the doorway, he took her into Jim's capacious office-cum-library where he sat in one of the large, upholstered armchairs and waited expectantly. She sat opposite him and took a notebook and pen out of her pocket. 'Just a few routine questions,' she said, 'although some of them may feel quite intrusive.'

'Fire away,' he said.

'I'd like to try and get a clearer picture of Jenny's state of mind when she left you in London. How was she? Did you have any reason to be alarmed by anything she said or did?'

'I confess I don't really know how she was inside. We never talked any more about our feelings but one thing happened before she left which did alarm me a bit.' And he went on to tell her briefly about the incident in Jane's bedroom. The policewoman took notes while he spoke.

'Thank you for that. Can I turn now to the note she left behind? First, I presume you've seen it?'

'Actually, no, I haven't but my father-in-law read it to me over the phone.'

'Do you remember exactly what it said?'

'Pretty much, I think.'

'In it she said and I quote, "my marriage is clearly in a terminal state". Would you agree with that?'

'Yes, I suppose I'd have to.'

'Would you mind telling me why?'

'Well, for one thing, we haven't had sex since before Jonathan was born,' he said brutally, trying to shock her.

But she was imperturbable and just continued writing. 'Was there any other reason why?'

'Not that I can think of off the top of my head,' he said blushing and thinking of Jane. 'I already told you that we'd stopped communicating years ago.'

'Did these problems have anything to do with Jonathan's condition?'

'I'm honestly not sure but I suspect that, deep down, she blamed me for it.'

'Well, thank you very much for your cooperation, Mr Spiller,' she said, getting up and closing her notebook. 'That will be all for now.'

'When do you think we might hear some news?'

Now it was her turn to be brutally frank and honest. 'Well, if she did commit suicide by jumping off one of the nearby cliffs, there is no telling when the body might turn up. The currents in this part of the North Sea can be ferocious. But, on the other hand, she might turn up later on today if she got wedged in a crevice. But you must be positive. Perhaps she's just wandered off to be alone somewhere. I imagine it must really take it out of one to have to look after a little boy like Jonathan full time.'

'Are you so frank with everybody?' David asked now, really wanting to know the answer.

'If you'd been the one to disappear and the mother claimed to have a happy marriage, I would have treated her with kid gloves,' she said.

David felt thoroughly rebuked by this remark and stood up to say goodbye. But then her mobile phone trilled. She looked at the number and turned to him, saying, 'Is there somewhere private I can take this?'

'Of course. I'll leave you alone in here.'

As he went out, closing the door, he heard her talking to one of her colleagues but couldn't make out the subject of the conversation. There was only the faint rumble of a man's voice on the other end. But a couple of minutes later she came out and said, 'I'm afraid I have some very bad news. They have found a woman's body under the cliffs and fear it could be your wife's.'

Then the reality of it all hit David and he felt all the blood drain from his head. He swayed, almost fainting with the shock. Rose came up to him at once and, supporting him by the arm, took him back into the office, seating him gently back in the same chair he'd been sitting in earlier. She noticed the drinks displayed in a cabinet and went over and poured him a large glass of cognac without asking for permission. He drained it gratefully and then spluttered as the fiery liquid burnt its way down into his stomach. 'Thanks for that,' he said as he felt the blood returning to his face. 'I think I'll be OK now.'

'Good,' she said, 'because I still have to ask you to do something and it might be the most difficult thing you'll ever have to do.'

'Go on,' he said.

'I'm afraid I'll have to ask you to accompany me to the mortuary to identify the body. I really can't ask either of her parents to do it. The shock might just kill them.'

THE END?

'OK. I'll do it. I know it's essential and I'd already prepared myself for something like this.'

'Thank you. We can leave whenever you're ready.'

'I'll just go and tell them I've got to go somewhere with you. It won't take long, will it? I won't tell them the news.'

'Good man and no, I shouldn't think so.'

So David went into the kitchen where his parents-in-law were just sitting in silence with Jonathan playing at their feet and told them he had to go out for a bit. He stressed he wouldn't be long and took his leave before they could ask him any questions.

CHAPTER 15

David got into the police car, which was standing in the road outside Jim and Madeleine's house, and Rose at once started the engine and drove off in the direction of Scarborough city centre. Tactfully, she didn't try to make conversation but left David to his thoughts and fears. He was mentally bracing himself for the task ahead but after a few minutes he asked her where the mortuary was. She told him it was in the main hospital in the city and, as he didn't know Scarborough very well, he asked no more questions. Just travelling in a police car was a novel experience for him and under different circumstances he might have enjoyed it but, as it was, he hardly noticed.

All too soon, however, they were pulling up outside an extension to a big hospital where

THE END?

Rose parked. She turned to look at him and said, 'Are you sure you're up to this?'

'I thought I had to be,' he replied bitterly, getting out of the police car. He'd never been inside a mortuary before but all the bustle and smells just inside the main doors reminded him strongly of a normal hospital like the one Jonathan had been born in and later treated at in London. It didn't smell of death, which he'd expected, although he really had no idea what death smelt like. He'd never been a soldier. The only thing different about it was the lack of patients. There were no wheelchairs in evidence or bandaged people, only trolleys.

There waiting for them was a more senior colleague of Rose's, who introduced himself as Superintendant Williams and greeted him by name, saying, 'I'm terribly sorry we have to put you through this, sir, but the sooner it's done, the sooner it'll be over. However, we have to wait until we're paged as they're still tidying the lady up.' David just nodded at these words, not really understanding them. His ability to process English seemed to have deserted him. Then the Superintendant continued, 'Thank you for bringing him, Rose. You can go now. If you could start writing up your report, that would be useful. I'll see Mr

Spiller home.' Rose nodded herself at these final remarks and then said goodbye to David before leaving with a long, sympathetic look at him. He was sorry she was leaving.

'How long are we going to have to wait? It's just that I told my parents-in-law I'd be back soon,' David asked, sitting down heavily on a nearby chair.

'They promised me no more than,' and here he looked at his watch, 'another 15 minutes or so.'

They sat in silence for a while, the Superintendant glancing at his watch from time to time, but then he was hailed by the receptionist who said, 'They're ready for you now.' The Superintendant got up and ushered David through a pair of swing doors and down a long corridor, stopping only when they reached a door marked just with a number. He knocked and a doctor in green scrubs opened it. 'Come in,' he said.

They went in and David found himself in a kind of vestibule with a number of chairs and a closed door on the other side. He and the Superintendant were then asked to change into their own scrubs which the doctor handed

THE END?

to them, including a pair of plastic overshoes and a mask. Then the doctor asked, 'Does your wife have any distinguishing marks? Tattoos maybe?'

David had to think hard – he hadn't seen his wife's naked body for so long – but he finally said, 'Yes, she has a small tattoo of a horse on the inside of her right thigh,' his voice sounding slightly muffled through the mask. Then he added irrelevantly, 'She had it done soon after we got married.'

'Thank you, sir. That's perfect,' the doctor said, as if David had just passed an exam with flying colours. Then he disappeared through the closed door but came out again almost immediately. 'If you'd like to follow me now, sir,' and the three of them went through the door and into a big room which smelled strongly of what David assumed was formaldehyde. David recognised the room at once from watching many police shows on TV. It was very brightly lit with a number of what were clearly big, stainless steel, pullout drawers at one end and in the middle of the floor was a single table with a form on it, draped in a white sheet. There were, however, no signs of bodily organs lying around like in the TV shows – everything was spotlessly clean. There were a couple of other doctors standing around, one of them, to his surprise, female, and the word 'pathologist' suddenly popped into his head. Yes, that was what they were called. David felt inordinately proud of himself for remembering the word. But he still hadn't – or was it couldn't? - focus on the form lying under the sheet.

The doctor who'd brought them in led them both round to the other side of the table and David forced himself to look at what was on it. But, although it was clearly a body, it was still covered in the sheet and couldn't be seen. David found his arm being gripped firmly by the police officer and was glad of the support. Then the doctor carefully lifted away the sheet and David gasped. There was his wife, looking as if she was just sleeping rather than dead! She was lying on her back and David could see no sign of injury at all. There was no blood to be seen. She was naked and her hair was wet– those were the only strange things about her.

Then the policeman said, 'Please can you confirm for us if this is your wife, sir?' David nodded but without replying. He didn't trust himself to speak. 'I'm sorry, sir, but you have to say the words.'

THE END?

'Yes, that's her,' he said, turning away, his eyes suddenly full of tears.

'Thank you, sir. I'm very sorry for your loss,' the policeman said and he firmly but gently led David away and back to the vestibule area where David numbly took off his scrubs. Then they were suddenly outside again with David having no memory of how they got there. He climbed into the front of Williams' car and they left the hospital, the policeman driving slowly.

'When will the body be released?' David asked after a while.

'After the autopsy,' the Superintendant replied. 'Probably within a couple of days.'

'OK,' David said before relapsing into silence again. Later he couldn't remember whether any other words passed between them on the journey.

When they arrived back at his parents-in-laws' house, the policeman turned to him and said, 'Would you like me to come in and help to break the news?'

David had to think about this but finally said, 'No, I'll manage on my own but thanks for the suggestion,' and the policeman just shrugged. But then he had an idea, 'I think, however, that it might be good if Rose was here. At least they've met her and she'll know better than me how to deal with Madeleine.'

'Yes, I agree. OK. I can organise that.' So he rang Rose, who David presumed was still at the police station, and he heard her say, 'Sure. I'll be right over.'

They had to wait about another 20 minutes for her to show up, during which time they sat in silence in the police car, David not thinking at all about anything – his brain seemed to have died along with Jenny. But then the Superintendant left, after thanking David again for his help, and he and Rose went up to the house.

When they went in, Madeleine came rushing up to them, saying accusingly to David, 'You've been gone so long!' but then she must have noticed David's expression and said, 'It's bad news, isn't it?'

David put his arms around his mother-in-law and said, 'I'm afraid so, Madeleine.'

THE END?

She promptly burst into tears and through them whispered, 'Is there any chance of a mistake?'

'I'm sorry but no,' David replied, trying his best to keep his own tears at bay.

'Well then, we'll have to tell Jim, won't we?' drying her eyes perfunctorily and being almost instantly transformed into a woman of action. David was astonished by the transformation, which just confirmed his feeling that he'd never understand women, and followed her into the kitchen where Jim was still sitting and staring into space. There was no sign of Jonathan and David assumed he'd gone down for his nap. Madeleine went up to him and, cupping his face in her hand and looking directly into his eyes, said, 'I'm afraid it's bad news, darling.'

Jim just looked up at her and said, 'So Jenny's dead, is she?' and his wife nodded. But then he seemed to go to pieces right in front of David and Rose, who were looking on helplessly. He started crying as if he'd never stop and kept on apologising for his tears, saying, 'Sorry. I'm so sorry.' Madeleine finally took her husband by the arm and led him meekly upstairs, presumably to put him to bed.

When she came down, she found David with his head on the kitchen table and Rose still just standing there, not having said a word so far. He could have been asleep but she knew he wasn't. 'David', she said. 'You're going to have to be the man of the house now and take care of all the practicalities. I'm going to be too busy with Jim and Jonathan.'

He looked up at her and said in a firmer voice than he'd felt he'd be able to muster, 'Of course, Madeleine. I'll do whatever's necessary.'

'Perhaps you could take Rose, isn't it, somewhere quiet to discuss them as I wouldn't know where to start.'

'Sure. Let's go back to the office, shall we?' and he led the way out of the kitchen, pleased that he'd actually been given something to do. It might keep him from crying.

Rose dutifully followed him and, when they were alone, said, 'Your mother-in-law is one tough cookie, isn't she?'

'I guess so although I've never really thought of her as one. So where do I start with the "practicalities"?' clearly putting the word into inverted commas.

'The first thing to organise is probably the funeral. You'll have a little while before the body's released and then, if you need longer, it can stay at the mortician's. Was she religious?'

'No. She never went to church in all the time I knew her.'

'Then cremation is probably the best option. Cheaper too. I'll e-mail you a list of the local crematoria as soon as I get back.' And now she took out her notebook and started scribbling. 'Did she leave a will?'

'Yes but it's in London.'

'OK. That's good too. It makes things much simpler all round. It doesn't matter where it is but you should probably inform her solicitor sooner rather than later. Did you have the same one, by the way?'

'Well, we made our wills together immediately after Jonathan was born so, unless she's changed hers, the answer is yes again. But to answer your next question, I'm afraid I don't have his number up here and don't think I can even remember his name.'

'Oh, well. When you next go down to London, don't forget to do it as many of the practical things can be sorted out by him. You'll also need to inform her bank so that they can close any accounts she might have.'

'OK. I've got all that. What else? I haven't had to do any of this stuff since my parents died and that was ages ago.'

'For most of the legal stuff you'll need copies of the death certificate but that should come through quite quickly, probably straight after the autopsy.'

'Why does she need an autopsy? It's clear enough how she died, isn't it?'

'Yes, to you maybe but the authorities will need to run toxicology and other tests to see if her mind could have been affected by anything. I'm afraid it's mandatory for any suspected suicide.'

'Oh, OK,' David said, shocked by her casual use of the word 'suicide'. But he knew that was what it was.

THE END?

'I'm afraid there might also be the need for an inquest. But that will depend on the coroner and you shouldn't need to go. Now, what else? Oh, yes. Did she have any insurance policies?'

'I'm not sure but I think so.'

'OK. You need to pass them onto the solicitor. He can deal with all that.'

'Do insurance policies pay out in the event of a suicide?' There! *He'd* said the word now. Perhaps he was at last getting used to the idea of what his wife had actually done.

'Most don't, it's true, but the solicitor will need to read their terms.'

'I seem to remember after my parents died being given a long list of things I had to do.'

'Yes, that's a good point. I'll see if I can dig one up for you. Can you give me your e-mail address now so I can send you the stuff about the local crematoria?'

'Sure.' And he read it out to her. Everything seemed to be happening much too quickly and he wasn't at all sure how much more he could take before breaking down completely.

'I'll come back and see how you're all getting on tomorrow if that's OK? I don't think there's anything else I can help you with now. Try and stay busy. It'll keep your mind off things. But you've got Jonathan, haven't you, to help you do that.'

Jonathan! In all the pressure of everything that had happened, he'd almost forgotten about his son! He got up guiltily and said, 'Yes, you're quite right about him. I ought to go and see how he's getting on. Thanks for all your help and see you tomorrow.' But she waved aside his thanks and then left.

∽

David at once went in search of Jonathan and found him playing in his nursery, totally oblivious of everything that was going on around him and being watched over by Madeleine, who appeared to be almost completely normal. When he saw his father, he jumped up and toddled over to him, something he had recently learnt to do. 'Dada!' he said happily and threw his arms around his neck. David squeezed him so hard he got a disapproving look from Madeleine but eventually put him down to go on playing.

THE END?

'Can we have a word?' he said to Madeleine and she followed him out of the nursery. Outside he said, 'There are quite a few things that need to be sorted out. But don't worry. I'll take care of them. There is one thing I need to ask you though. Would it be OK for Jenny to be cremated?'

'Yes, of course. That'll be fine,' she replied. 'I know Jim won't care.'

'Good. Thanks. Would you mind looking after Jonathan for a while longer while I deal with stuff?'

'No. You go right ahead.'

So David left her, thinking of priorities, and suddenly remembered something urgent. He had to phone his office! They would be wondering where he was. So he rang them immediately and explained to his boss what had happened. She was most sympathetic and told him to take off as much time as he needed. 'And please don't worry about money,' she said. 'We'll keep on paying your salary for as long as it takes.' He said his thanks, putting down the phone with relief, and then thought to look at his e-mails. Amongst all the rubbish, there was one already from Rose with an attachment. He opened it and saw it was the list of local crematoria as she'd promised with addresses and phone numbers. He reckoned he needed at least to ring, if not visit, a couple of them to see what they had to offer and how long they would take to carry out the funeral.

So, after looking them up on his Google map, he rang the nearest one to the house on the list and told them that his wife had just died unexpectedly and he wanted to have her cremated. The lady he spoke to sounded very nice but said there'd probably be a couple of weeks' delay before they could cremate her. 'How much would it cost?' he asked now and she mentioned a price which staggered him but said that it depended on the type of coffin and included the services of a preacher too and a memorial plaque in their garden. 'Thank you,' he said. 'I'll get back to you.' Was Jenny going to bankrupt him by dying so unexpectedly? But he put the thought aside as unworthy.

Then he rang the second on the list and got almost exactly the same spiel with a very similar price attached. So at least now he had a ballpark figure although he knew it would probably be much more expensive in London.

THE END?

He remembered his idea of going to visit a couple of them to inspect them personally and decided to ask Madeleine if he could borrow their car.

But then he looked at his watch and saw it was nearly dinner time, much too late to go visiting. He needed to eat as he hadn't had any food at all since breakfast and was very hungry. He wondered where the day had gone and then it all came rushing back to him and he began to feel very despondent and almost sorry for himself. How could Jenny have done this not only to her parents and him but, most of all, to Jonathan? But he knew no answers would be forthcoming. The words he had heard in a million cop shows came back to him: "whilst the balance of her mind was disturbed" and wondered if they would be used to describe his wife. Could he have done anything differently? On balance he decided no although his guilt over Jane rankled more and more. Jenny simply couldn't have found out about them, could she? And, even if she had, surely that wouldn't be enough to tip her over the edge, would it? Again there were too many questions and not enough answers.

So he gave up on his speculations and went in search of his mother-in-law. He found her in the kitchen feeding Jonathan, who was tucking in happily. 'Any chance of some food?' he asked after giving his son another fierce cuddle and getting his yoghurt all over the front of his shirt, which made Jonathan laugh.

'Give me a few minutes to finish him and I'll make some supper,' she replied.

'OK. I'll go up and have a quick shower and get changed,' he said.

The two of them ate dinner in silence and alone without Jim, who he presumed was still sleeping although he didn't ask Madeleine about him. Afterwards he felt very tired, remembering he'd had very little sleep the night before and thinking that all the shocks of the day must have worn him out. He decided to go up to bed as there was nothing else useful he could accomplish till the morning and somehow managed to sleep surprisingly well in the comfortable spare bed, certainly much better than he had on the sofa the previous night, even though his sleep was disturbed by several nightmares which, mercifully, he couldn't remember the next morning.

CHAPTER 16

The following morning at breakfast David asked Madeleine if Jonathan had asked yet about his mother and she said that she'd told him she'd had to go away for a few days, an answer which seemed to satisfy him. She reminded him how infinitely adaptable young children were and he was relieved. As long as at least one of his parents or grandparents was around, he seemed perfectly happy. Then David asked if he could borrow their car as he needed to run some errands and Madeleine at once gave him the key. He finally saw Jim before he left, looking about twenty years older than he had but at least he seemed to have recovered somewhat from the shock.

So, after giving Jonathan another big cuddle and telling him that he had to go out for a while, he left the house to visit the crematoria. Both of the ones he had phoned yesterday seemed OK to him but one was better tended with a really lovely garden, so he decided to go with that one. When he told the supervisor this, she asked what kind of service he would like.

'What can you offer?' he asked.

'We can do almost any religion and we have a humanist pastor who comes in to help out when needed.' The sound of a humanist funeral appealed to David and he asked now if it would be possible to meet the pastor. 'Yes, of course. She always insists on meeting a member of the family anyway to find out as much as she can about the deceased. Don't forget also it would be good to have some suggestions for music to be played as well.'

He promised to think about this and after setting up a potential date for the funeral and leaving his phone number, he left and went back to the house. When he got there, he found Rose's police car parked outside and Madeleine closeted with Rose in the kitchen. She was holding his mother-in-law's hand and talking seriously but jumped up as soon as David came in. 'How are you?' she asked.

THE END?

'Keeping busy as you suggested,' he replied, somewhat enigmatically. But then he realised Madeleine needed to be kept in the loop so he started to talk about what he'd achieved so far and what still had to be done. 'It looks like the funeral will probably be held in a couple of weeks, which should give you enough time to sort out who you want to invite,' he said, looking at Madeleine.

'Yes, I've already started to think about that,' she replied. 'But it will probably be just family members, those who can actually make it.'

'Whatever,' David said, realising that he'd never met any other members of Jenny's family.

'You seem to have done an awful lot in a very short time,' Rose commented but he just grunted in reply. 'Anyway, I came over not only to see how you were getting on but also to bring you this,' and she presented him with a leaflet.

He glanced at it and realised it was the list of things that needed to be done after somebody had died. 'Thanks a lot, Rose. This should be very helpful,' he said.

'I was talking to Madeleine when you came in about the possibility of getting council help for Jonathan if he's going to be here for a while and also counselling for herself and Jim,' Rose said now.

'I told her I was quite worried about Jim although right now he's playing with Jonathan upstairs which he always enjoys,' Madeleine said.

'That's an excellent idea,' David said. Then he asked Rose 'Is this all part of your duties?'

She laughed and replied, 'I guess you could say that,' which didn't really answer his question but satisfied him nonetheless. He would have felt guilty if he knew she was just doing it out of the kindness of her heart.

'I'll probably need to go back to London soon to sort out Jenny's business there and her personal possessions,' David said now, feeling that the latter task was probably beyond him but knowing it had to be done.

'That's fine,' Madeleine said. 'We should be able to cope here.' And then Rose left, saying that she'd organised it so that the death certificate would be sent to Madeleine's house, which David was grateful for, and that she

THE END?

was available any time if they needed more help with anything.

'She's really very sweet, isn't she?' Madeleine said and David agreed, wondering what he could do now to 'keep busy'. But then Madeleine said, 'It's almost lunchtime. Could you help with laying the table?' which solved that problem, if only in the very short-term.

They all ate lunch together, with Jonathan happily slurping up his food, clearly pleased to have his father there, and then he went down for his nap. David thought he might as well take the opportunity while his son was sleeping to return to London so he took a taxi to the station, having looked up the train times, and left, telling Madeleine and Jim he'd drive back the next day in his own car.

He spent the journey time reading the leaflet Rose had left him and making a list of all he had to do on his return home. It was a long list. He got back home in the late afternoon and, after looking up the telephone numbers in his filing cabinet, started to make his business calls, fortunately managing to get through each time. He told his solicitor, who offered his sincere condolences, about the death certificate which should arrive in

Scarborough sometime soon and was asked to fax photocopies to him. The bank told him not to worry yet about any debts Jenny might have had. They would all be sorted out in the fullness of time. All in all, it was quite a productive afternoon with everybody he spoke to being very helpful.

When he'd finished, he sat back in his armchair and wondered if he'd dare call Jane. He knew she had the right to know what had happened so hesitantly he dialled her number. She picked up almost at once and said, 'So what news of Jenny, David?' and he poured out a brief synopsis of the terrible story to her. She was shocked into uncharacteristic silence when he stopped, only managing to murmur, 'How dreadful!' But then, after a few seconds' pause, she found her voice and said 'And what about you?'

He knew what she meant and replied, 'I'm doing OK, thanks, at the moment anyway.'

'Do you want to come round?'

'Sorry. I can't. I've far too much to do here.'

'OK. Well, when you do, you know where I am.'

THE END?

'Thanks, Jane. You're a real brick.' And then he hung up, emotionally exhausted by the call. It was the first time he'd spoken to anybody about the details of the suicide and now, surrounded by the detritus of his and Jenny's lives together, he began to remember all the good times they'd had, the last three years seeming to fade into insignificance. But he knew he couldn't break down – not yet. There simply wasn't time. So he set to the task of getting Jenny's personal stuff together and filled a couple of suitcases with it, not bothering with her clothes, however. He just put in what he thought Jim and Madeleine might like to keep, including her laptop. Then he packed a couple more suitcases with clothes for himself, including his best suit which he knew he'd have to wear for the funeral, and after a quick bite to eat from the remnants of what was left in the house and a glass of wine, he finally collapsed into bed in the spare room, certainly not wanting to sleep in his marital bed. At first, however, he couldn't sleep but buried his head in the pillow and wept properly for the first time for his dead wife and her wasted life.

He still hadn't given a thought to what the future might hold for himself and Jonathan.

CHAPTER 17

The next morning David woke up very early, his pillow still wet from the tears of the night before. But he felt stronger now as if those tears had purged him of something. He thought of ringing Jane again but decided against it on the grounds that he didn't know what to say or, rather, to add to what he'd already said. So, after ringing Madeleine and telling her he'd be leaving soon and having a couple of cups of strong coffee, he got the car out, put the suitcases in and started the long drive back to Scarborough.

It took him nearly five hours to get there, as opposed to three on the train, mainly because of the heavy traffic but he made it without incident, pulling up finally with relief into his parents-laws' driveway. He went into the house and found Madeleine in the kitchen

THE END?

with Jonathan playing happily at her feet. He was given the usual rapturous welcome by his son and then sat at the table and asked if there was anything to eat.

'You can have left-overs if that's OK,' Madeleine said. David agreed that was fine and quickly a large bowl of home-made soup was put before him which he devoured ravenously. 'When did you last eat?' Madeleine asked him critically and he had to think.

'Last night I had a quick bite at home,' he admitted.

'You've got to look after yourself,' she said and he smiled at her motherly solicitousness. She brought him some more food which he polished off equally quickly and then sat back on his chair saying, 'That's better. Thanks a lot, Madeleine.' He looked at his watch and then said, 'Isn't it about time for Jonathan's nap?'

'Yes but I was waiting for you to come back,' Madeleine said now, picking his son up in her arms and leaving the kitchen. David thought to himself how lucky he was to have such a loving mother-in-law but then grimaced, remembering the criticism he'd levelled at Jenny for being so close to her parents. He felt thoroughly guilty about that now. Guilt seemed to be becoming an integral part of his life at present.

Madeleine soon returned and, sitting herself opposite him, asked without preamble, 'So did you do everything you wanted to do in London?'

'All the important stuff anyway,' he replied.

Then she picked up a piece of paper that had been lying on the counter and passed it to him. He looked at it and at once saw that it was Jenny's death certificate. 'Look at the cause of death,' she said. So he did and then whistled. It said: *"Accidental fall from cliff top near Scarborough Point".* 'It just arrived this morning,' Madeleine said now. 'I guess it's quite good news, isn't it?'

'Yes, indeed, even if we know it's not true. But I suppose there is no absolute proof she didn't fall.'

'No, exactly. But it should simplify things when it comes to insurance policies and stuff like that, shouldn't it? And it also makes it much easier to tell people, I suppose.'

'Yes. Absolutely.' He paused and then asked, 'Has Jim seen this?'

'Yes. He was the one to open the envelope. I think it made him very sad as it's so final. He's in bed as we speak. He collapsed when he read it.'

'Oh, no! That's terrible! You'll have to be strong for him, Madeleine.'

'Oh, don't worry about me. Us women are tougher than we look.'

'I've come to appreciate that,' David said, thinking, however, that Jenny hadn't been very tough but not saying anything more on the subject. Then he got up from the table and, picking up the death certificate, said, 'Well, I've got lots of things to do so I'll leave you in peace. See you later.' And he left the kitchen.

First he went out to the car and brought in the suitcases, taking his own up to his room and leaving Jenny's in the hallway for Madeleine to deal with, telling her they were there. Then he took the death certificate into Jim's study and, after scanning it onto his computer, e-mailed off a few copies to his solicitor in London. After that he rang Rose and when he managed to get through, said, 'Did you have anything to do with the death certificate mentioning the cause of death as an accident?'

But she was horrified at the suggestion and said, 'No! Certainly not!' But then she continued more calmly, 'I presume it was because the doctors had no proof she'd committed suicide and it was simpler and kinder to put it down as an accident. But it's better for you, isn't it?'

'Yes, of course. And that's what Madeleine and I presumed too.'

'And it means also that there should be no necessity for an inquest.'

'I hadn't thought of that. Well, anyway, thanks a lot for all your help. I've been down to London and started to sort things out with her solicitor and her bank and hope that everything's now under control.'

'Good for you. Well done! I'd like to come to the funeral if I may. Could you ask Madeleine if that would be OK?'

'Yes, of course. I'm sure it will but I'll certainly ask her.'

THE END?

'Have you thought about your own future now with Jonathan?'

'No, not really. I guess I'll just have to wait and see. It depends on so many things.'

'Yes, I suppose it does. Don't forget to ring me any time, even if you just want to talk.'

'Thanks again, Rose. You've totally renewed my faith in Her Majesty's Constabulary,' at which she just laughed and hung up. He thought about what else he needed to do but, apart from the funeral arrangements which he was now leaving mostly to Madeleine, there's wasn't anything urgent he could think of but he knew that he *had* to keep busy if he wasn't going to fall to pieces. This was not the time for introspection.

Then, however, he heard the phone go in the hall and Madeleine answer it. She at once brought it into him saying, 'It's about her body. I thought you should deal with it.'

He listened and heard a voice say, 'Is that Mr Spiller?'

'Yes, that's me.'

'This is the mortuary, sir. We are now ready to release your wife's body. Where would you like it to be taken?'

This was something he hadn't considered and he had to think quickly. 'Is there a mortician somewhere near where I am?' he asked and gave his parents-in-laws' address.

'Let me look it up, sir, but there's no urgency. She can stay here if you wish. Can you hold the line?' the voice said. David waited a minute or two and then the voice came back, 'The nearest one to you is a couple of miles away but I wouldn't really recommend it. There's another, much better one a bit further away, called Millers.'

'Thanks. Can you give me their phone number and I'll get back to you.'

'No problem, sir.' And he rattled off a number, which David copied down, and then gave him his own number at the mortuary.

David at once rang the mortician and got through straight away. 'My name is Mr Spiller,' he said, 'and my wife was recently killed in a fall. I've been recommended to you by the mortuary who are ready to release her body. Could you take her?'

'I'm so very sorry,' said a female and youngish-sounding voice sympathetically. 'Let me just check.' There was another short wait until the voice came back. 'Yes, sir. We have room.'

'Great. I'll tell the mortuary to send her body straight to you then. If you could ring me back when you receive her, I'll come straight over with all the details you need and payment of course.' And he gave her his mobile number.

'That's fine, sir. If you'd like to bring any of her favourite clothes when you come and anything you'd like her to have in her coffin at the funeral, that would be helpful.'

'Sure. I'll do that. Could you give me your address?' She did so and he hung up before ringing the mortuary back. 'Everything's arranged with Millers,' he said and the man on the other end said, 'Gosh! That was quick! OK. We'll send the body there at once if you'd like us to.'

'You might as well.' David said and that was the end of the conversation. He went to find Madeleine and heard her voice coming from her bedroom talking quietly to Jim. She came out as soon as he knocked and he said, 'I need to talk to you for a moment.'

She followed him outside and he told her what he'd done but adding that he'd need to choose some clothes for Jenny and, possibly, something personal to put in her coffin. 'Are you happy for me to do that?'

'Yes, of course, David. That's fine,' she said. So he went downstairs to where he'd left Jenny's suitcases with all her personal stuff inside and brought them up to his own, spare bedroom. He already knew what he was looking for to put in her coffin and found it quickly – an ancient teddy bear which Jenny had told him once she'd had since she was a child and which she had kept on her bedside table ever since David had known her. Her clothes were a more difficult problem but he went into her bedroom which was next to Jonathan's nursery and opened the wardrobe. And, feeling awful while he did it, he took out a number of dresses and finally found one which was quite pretty and which he didn't remember her having and thought it would do. Then he chose some panties and a bra from the chest of drawers and finally a pair of decent shoes from the bottom of the wardrobe. He hoped that was everything the mortician would need but reckoned he could always come back to the house any time if he'd forgotten anything. He put the clothes and shoes into one of Jenny's suitcases after emptying it in her room, along with the teddy bear, and carried it downstairs to his car where he looked up the address of the mortician on his Satnav and keyed it in.

That was about all he could do for now so he went back into the house and decided to have a nap of his own. He was feeling tired after everything he'd done already that day. So he went up to his room and lay down, making sure his phone was nearby. He fell asleep almost immediately and was only woken by its trilling. Blearily he picked it up and said, 'Hello.'

'Is that Mr Spiller?' the same girl's voice asked who he'd spoken to earlier from the mortician's.

'Yes. Have you got her?' he said, fully awake now.

'Yes, she's just arrived. You can view her whenever you want.'

'Thank you. I'll be bringing some clothes for her and other stuff. See you soon.' And he hung up and went into the adjoining bathroom to wash his face. Then he looked at his watch and saw with amazement that it was three hours since he'd lain down. It was now early evening. I must have been more tired than I'd reckoned, he thought to himself.

He went downstairs and found Madeleine in the kitchen preparing supper, with Jonathan playing on the floor as usual. 'I have to go out for a bit but I shouldn't be too long,' he told her.

'OK. We'll have supper whenever you return,' Madeleine said without asking any questions.

So he went outside, got into his car and drove off. He found the mortician's without any trouble and went inside. The girl he'd spoken to had gone off duty but he found a nice, smartly dressed young man who was expecting him.

'Would you like to see your wife?' he asked first but David shook his head, saying, 'No, thank you. Not right now. I've just come to bring you her stuff and deal with the paperwork.' And he handed over the suitcase with Jenny's clothes in it.

THE END?

'As you wish, sir.' And they got right down to it.

First David had to choose a coffin from a catalogue, which he did quite quickly on the young man's recommendation, wincing at the price. Then he dealt with a few other funeral arrangements, making quick decisions on the spot, and was asked if he knew the date of the funeral yet. He admitted that he didn't know exactly but assumed it would be held in the next couple of weeks.

'That's fine, sir. She can stay here as long as necessary. Do you wish the coffin to be open or closed?'

David thought for a second and then decided, 'Closed, please.' He didn't want Jim or Madeleine having to go through the ordeal of actually seeing their dead daughter.

'And where will the funeral be held?' and David told him the name of the crematorium. The young man, who had been taking notes on everything David told him, finally said, 'Well, I think that's the lot, sir. If you could just give me your credit card now, I'll take the details but you won't be billed anything until after the funeral and then only assuming you're happy with everything.'

'Thank you very much,' David said, handing it over, but then, before he left, he remembered the teddy bear and told the young man to put it in the coffin, who made a final note, saying, 'Will do. As soon as you have a date for the funeral, please let us know. Oh and don't forget we're open all day seven days a week so if you want to change any of the arrangements, just give us a ring.' And David promised he would on both counts, pleased with the service he'd received. Then with a final handshake he left.

As he was driving back to the house, David decided he really felt like getting drunk that night, hoping that, although this was something he very rarely did, it might help him to forget everything at least for a short time. So he stopped off at an off license near the house and bought himself a bottle of gin and a couple of large bottles of tonic water. He carried the bottles guiltily into the house and up to his room and then came down to the kitchen where Jim and Madeleine were waiting for him to arrive. Jonathan was there too, clearly having eaten already, and squealed a welcome before returning to his Lego bricks.

THE END?

After a light supper, during which the adults talked hardly at all, not asking him even where he'd been, David took Jonathan up to his room and put him to bed after reading him one of his favourite stories, which was almost a novelty for him. Then he went back to his own room and, taking his toothbrush glass, proceeded to work his way through the gin until he finally collapsed onto his bed into a dreamless sleep. He woke up once in the middle of the night with a pounding headache, a raging thirst and a desperate urge to pee but, having forced himself up to urinate and have a glass of water, went back to sleep again.

CHAPTER 18

The next morning David got up very early, feeling pretty ghastly, but knew that the gin had done the trick of letting him sleep. He staggered downstairs and forced himself to have some breakfast along with several cups of coffee and a couple of Paracetamol, which made him feel better. Nobody else seemed to be up yet. Then he thought to look at his phone for messages and there was one that he opened immediately. It was from a Mrs Fitzgerald, the humanist pastor, who said that she was looking forward to talking to him and left her number.

It was still early but he rang the number and got through at once. A pleasant-sounding woman answered and he asked if he was talking to Ms Fitzgerald.

THE END?

'Yes. This is she. What can I do for you?'

'My name is David Spiller and my wife's just been killed in a terrible accident. I was hoping you might be able to officiate at her funeral.' Short and to the point, he thought.

'Oh yes, the crematorium told me about you and I was expecting you to call. I would be very happy to do so if you're sure.'

'Can we meet?' he asked.

'Yes. We need to anyway. Could you make it over to my place, do you think?'

'Yes, I could certainly do that.'

'When would you like to come?'

'Today some time?'

'By all means. How about later on this morning? I don't have anything on today. Shall we say 11 o'clock?'

'Yes, that would be fine. Could you give me your address?' And she told him slowly while he wrote it down.

'OK. See you later then.' And he hung up. Another thing to keep him busy, he thought sadly. He knew she would want details of Jenny's life and achievements and decided to write down as well as he could a kind of short biography of her. It would be helpful for himself too, he hoped. So he went back up to his room, tidied himself up and started typing on his laptop. As the memories came flooding back, he began to feel tearful and lost again but this time he didn't give in to them and just kept going. He started by describing their secondary school days together and then went on to discuss university and Jenny's accomplishments there before continuing with their jobs and a brief description of the next happy twenty years together and finished with Jonathan and what a wonderful mother she'd been to him. He read it through once, decided it would do and took it down to Jim's office to print it off. Then he went to find the rest of his family.

They were in the kitchen as he'd expected and he greeted them all, especially his son to whom he gave his standard cuddle. Jim hardly responded but Madeleine asked if he'd eaten and he said, 'Yes. Actually, I've been up for ages doing stuff. Which reminds me, I have to go out soon for an appointment. I hope that's OK?'

'Yes, of course. You do what you have to do, David,' Madeleine said, reminding him of Jane's words to him from what seemed like an age ago. But he couldn't think about *her* now. So, ruffling Jonathan's hair, he said, 'OK. I'll be off then.'

But then the doorbell went and David's heart sank as he answered it. Not more complications, he thought miserably. But it turned out to be one of his parents-in-laws' neighbours, who he'd never met and who introduced herself as Brenda, waving a copy of the local newspaper.

'This wouldn't be your wife, would it?' she asked, pointing at a headline which screamed "*Dead body found near the Point.*" He skimmed the article quickly and found it a reasonably accurate portrayal of what had happened with no mention of it being a potential suicide and without identifying Jenny.

'Yes, I'm afraid it would. How did you know?'

'Madeleine called me with the dreadful news yesterday. I'm so terribly sorry.'

'Thank you. Madeleine and Jim are both inside. I'm afraid I have to go out now.'

'OK. I won't detain you. Once again, please accept my condolences.'

'Thank you. Goodbye,' and he made his escape, thinking surely Jenny's death wouldn't be turned into a media circus. That would be intolerable. But he knew there was nothing he could do about it. He just hoped that Brenda wouldn't upset Jim too much if she showed him the article.

∼

He found his way to the pastor's house without problems, arriving more or less on time, and knocked. A middle-aged woman with a kindly face opened the door and said, 'Mr Spiller?'

'Yes, that's me. But do please call me David.'

'Thank you. And my name's Gloria. Nice to meet you. Come on in.' And she ushered him into a cosy living room and pointed to an armchair. 'Sit down and I'll just bring in the tea.' He'd forgotten how hospitable Yorkshire folk were, not a bit like Londoners, he thought wryly.

When they were settled, with David putting his tea on a small table nearby and balancing a plate with home-made biscuits on it on his knee, she said by way of preamble, 'First let me say how terribly sorry I am for your loss. How old was your wife?'

He had to think before answering. It was not a question he'd been asked recently. 'Forty two,' he said.

'Far too young,' she said, radiating sympathy, and David decided there and then that he liked her.

'Yes, I agree,' he said. 'I assume you'll want to ask me lots of questions about Jenny,' he continued and she nodded. 'I've written a little about her which might save some time.' And now he pulled from his jacket pocket the papers he'd printed out that morning in Jim's office.

'Thank you,' she said. 'May I read it now?'

'Yes, by all means,' David replied and sat back, munching on his biscuits and sipping his tea while she read it through.

'This is perfect,' she said when she'd finished. 'Many thanks for doing it.' But then she looked at him closely and added, 'But how are you doing?'

Under her gaze David felt a bit uncomfortable and wasn't sure how to respond. But then he said simply, 'Surviving, thanks.'

'Is that enough?' she asked now.

'No, not really. But it'll have to do for the moment, won't it?'

'If you say so,' she said, still scrutinising him closely.

'What's your day job, Gloria?' he asked now, eager to change the subject and realising suddenly that there were no signs of children or a partner in the house.

'I'm a bereavement counsellor,' she replied and he realised that was probably why she'd asked the question about how *he* was.

'Have you been through it yourself?'

'Yes, I have indeed. And I know how difficult it can be.'

THE END?

Then he said, 'Actually my father-in-law seems to have taken it very hard. I wonder if you'd agree to see him.'

'I'd be happy to talk to him. But the request must come from him.'

'OK. Well, I can only ask.' And he got up to go.

'Hang on a minute,' she said. 'We still haven't discussed the funeral itself.'

'Oh, yes. That's true,' he replied, wondering whether he'd deliberately been avoiding the subject and sitting down again.

So, very tactfully, she made a few suggestions, all of which David agreed to, including him saying a few words, and then asked him about music. He remembered then that the lady at the crematorium had asked him the same question but he hadn't considered it yet and admitted as much.

'Jenny wasn't particularly into music,' he said. 'What would you suggest?'

'Perhaps a part of a famous requiem,' she said.

'That sounds fine – Faure's perhaps? Can you set it up?'

'Yes, of course. Well, I think that's it then. Please let me know as soon as you have a date for the funeral,' she said, standing herself now. He promised he would and, shaking her hand, left, convinced that the funeral at least would be in good hands. On the way back he bought a copy of the local newspaper, interested to see whether it said anything else about Jenny. But, apart from an editorial complaining about the lack of safety precautions on the local cliff top paths, there was nothing.

CHAPTER 19

The next few days were a fallow period when David couldn't do much so he spent them mostly in the company of Jonathan, getting reacquainted with his overall schedule until he felt that, if necessary, he could look after him by himself. Madeleine was a great help with this, even showing him how to prepare his food. There was no repetition of the drinking episode and no reporters came to bother them.

Jim wasn't much in evidence at this time although he did appear at meals but said very little and when David told him about the offer from Gloria, he just said, 'We'll see.' Both Madeleine and David had to be content with this although his mother-in-law told him in private that she would keep on at Jim about it.

However, a date for the funeral was decided on by Madeleine quite quickly so David let all the principals know. It was due to happen on the Wednesday afternoon of the following week, less than ten days away. She had apparently invited everybody she wanted to and had asked David if there was anyone he wanted to invite too but he said no. There really was nobody he could think of he knew well enough to ask to come up from London except for Jane and he certainly didn't want her there. After the funeral, she told him, she'd asked everyone back to the house for tea and cakes.

David decided that the following Friday he would take Jonathan back to London with him and he told Madeleine this. He didn't want to be a burden on his parents-in-law any longer than he had to, even though he wasn't sure if they looked on him as a burden. But he knew it was time to return to the 'real' world and take control of his own life again. He also knew that there was still plenty of business to take care of in London. He'd been in touch with his solicitor who'd thanked him for the copies of the death certificate and told him that everything was now in train. The reading of the will could happen whenever he returned to London as it was very straightforward. He

THE END?

hadn't heard anything from Jane and wasn't sure if he felt relieved or sad.

But all too soon the day of the funeral arrived. Madeleine had arranged with Brenda, the neighbour, to look after Jonathan while it was happening. David dressed in his best suit, white shirt and tie and came downstairs, feeling faintly ridiculous. He had the notes of his short speech in his pocket even though he'd practised it until he knew it off by heart. He'd arranged to drive Jim and Madeleine in his car to the crematorium and they both came out of the house on time, smartly dressed although Jim still looked very care-worn.

They set off without talking and, when they arrived, David took his parents-in-law inside where he was gratified to see that the chapel was decorated with lots of flowers. There they met Gloria, who was dressed normally but smartly, not in a cassock, but, after only a few words with her, took their seats in a front row pew, waiting for the rest of the congregation to arrive. Some classical music, which David recognised but couldn't have put a name to, was playing quietly in the background. There were already a number of other people sitting down but David didn't know any of them except for Rose who was sitting just behind them, dressed now in civilian clothes. She smiled at him and he managed a small smile back. He was glad to see her there, a friendly face among all the strangers. The coffin glowed in a spotlight in front of them, the wood shining. They waited a while, reading the order of the service, which was printed with Jenny's name at the top, while more people arrived and then the service started.

Gloria started with an accurate tribute to Jenny's qualities, based on the notes he'd given her, and then asked him to come up and say a few words. He went up and stood awkwardly in front of the microphone for a few seconds before launching into his prepared speech. He talked about the happy times he and Jenny had had together, including a couple of anecdotes about things that had happened to them on holiday, and then a bit about the trauma of Jonathan's birth but how happy they'd been when he'd been born in spite of his disability. However, he didn't manage to finish it smoothly. A strangled sob came out of his mouth before the end and he felt everybody looking at him. Gloria put a gentle hand on his shoulder and this steadied him enough to be able to take his notes out of his pocket and finish. With absolutely no reason to, he felt very ashamed of himself. He had no idea

THE END?

what had just happened except that perhaps he missed Jenny more than he realised. But there was a smattering of applause when he finished and Gloria whispered to him, 'Well done!'

Then Gloria asked if anybody else had anything to say and Jim put up his hand. He got up and stood in front of the congregation, staring out bleakly at them. David hoped he wasn't going to make a fool of himself and break down but it was nothing like that. He started by thanking David for organising such a lovely funeral for his daughter, which made David blush but think savagely that if he hadn't *had* to do it, he would have gone completely round the bend. Then he went on to talk fluently and powerfully without notes about the pain of losing a child and several of the women there started sobbing, including Madeleine who was sitting next to David, and David himself felt his own tears returning. But then Jim changed tack and finished firmly, 'But I know, of course, that life must go on so goodbye, Jenny, wherever you are, and God bless you.' This was the first mention of God in the service and actually David thought it fitted in fine. When Jim sat down, everybody there stood up and started applauding him and David realised that he was the real star of the show. But he didn't begrudge him this. In fact, he was very happy for him.

Then Gloria asked everybody for a few moments' silent contemplation before she pushed a couple of buttons and the coffin trundled backwards and disappeared behind a curtain, there, David presumed, to be consumed by the flames. The sound of an organ filled the chapel with more classical music and Gloria led everybody outside to the garden where they all milled around in the sunshine, mainly wanting to congratulate Jim on his speech, although a few people did come up to David and offer their condolences. He also spoke briefly to Rose, inviting her back to the house, but she said she was going on duty soon. So he just said goodbye to her, thanking her again for everything she had done to help, and she wished him luck.

There was already a temporary plaque for Jenny on the wall next to hundreds of others and David thought how well everything had gone. He went up to Gloria and thanked her for the beautiful service, inviting her back to the house as well, but she also demurred, saying that she was too busy, and he didn't press her. He looked at his watch and saw that it was less than an hour since they'd arrived. A

THE END?

short but sweet send-off, he thought, exactly what he'd had in mind.

Then he went off in search of the administrator of the crematorium, finding her in her little office, and asked her if she wanted to be paid now for the service and she said, 'It's entirely up to you.' But David suddenly realised he probably wouldn't be back there again so he insisted on paying there and then and she took his credit card. Before he left, she said, 'You'll be able to collect your wife's ashes in a couple of days,' and David realised that this was one more thing he hadn't considered. He knew he didn't want to keep them in London and decided to ask Madeleine either to keep them herself or to scatter them somewhere appropriate. He hoped she'd be pleased with the gesture even though he was really doing it for himself.

And that was the end of the funeral. Afterwards most of the people who'd been there went back to the house where Brenda had laid out a fine spread of cakes and soft drinks. David was forced to socialise although he did get a reprieve when Jonathan woke up from his nap and started bawling and he brought him downstairs to meet everybody where they all made a big fuss of him. Jonathan himself, of course, had no idea what it was all about.

But then at last everybody left and they had supper together when Madeleine congratulated him on the smooth running of the funeral, which gratified him.

'Do you think Jenny would have approved?' he asked timidly now.

'Yes. I'm sure she would have done,' Madeleine replied and he had to be content with that.

Eventually he managed to put Jonathan, who was still rather over-excited by all the visitors to the house earlier, to bed and almost straight after that went to bed himself, emotionally shattered by the afternoon.

CHAPTER 20

David overslept the next morning and got up feeling slightly groggy but presumed he'd needed the sleep. So he washed and went downstairs in search of the family. As usual they were congregated in the kitchen with Jonathan playing on the floor and Jim on his hands and knees playing with him. He made himself some coffee and then asked if there was anything he could do. But Madeleine said no so he mooched on back to his bedroom and sat on the bed, wondering how he was going to fill the next 24 hours until he could leave. He was desperate now to get back to London.

But the day slowly passed with him only managing to take care of one piece of business, paying off the mortician's, and soon it was the following morning. David packed up his stuff and took it down to the car. Then he did the same with Jonathan's things and finally went back inside to say goodbye. He kissed Madeleine, thanking her for her hospitality, and shook Jim's hand. Jim said, 'If you ever need our help with Jonathan, just give us a call and we'll come a-running,' and David realised how much they were going to miss their grandson, especially as their beloved daughter was now gone.

Then he picked up Jonathan and, after strapping him into his car seat, looked back at his parents-in-law who were standing on the porch to wave him off. He waved himself, started the engine and drove off, knowing that a new phase of his life was about to begin.

He drove carefully back to London, mindful of his cargo and stopping for lunch on the way, and got home in the middle of the afternoon. He took Jonathan upstairs at once to his old room and put him down for a nap as he was tired after the long journey and hadn't slept much on the way, and then brought everything inside from the car. After unpacking it all, he went into the kitchen and decided to make a list of the food they needed. This kept him busy for a while as he had to throw out a lot of stuff from the fridge which was now long past its sell-by date.

THE END?

He'd been thinking about Jane the whole way back and wondered if he could ring her now and finally decided that it couldn't hurt. So he dialled her home number – he didn't have her mobile number - but only got her answering service so he just left a short message saying that he was back and asking her to give him a call. Then he thought to call his office, knowing that his boss would still be in as she was a workaholic and never left early on Fridays unlike most of the employees. He got through and told her that he was back in London but had no idea when he'd be able to return to work as it all depended on getting somebody in to look after Jonathan. She knew of his home situation with his son and was, as he'd expected, very sympathetic, just telling him to keep in touch. He was still on full pay and would remain so for quite a while yet so finances should not be a huge problem although he was worried about the size of his credit card bill.

He remembered to ring Madeleine to tell her he'd got back safely and then he just pottered around in the house until Jonathan woke up. Unsurprisingly, he seemed rather confused about where he was and asked in his own way where his mother was. He told him, as he remembered Madeleine had, that she'd had to go away for a while and that seemed to more or less satisfy him. However, David found it difficult to comfort him but he remembered Madeleine's words about how infinitely adaptable children were and took some reassurance from them. Then he went out with Jonathan in the car and did a big shop, getting enough food to last them for a while. But Jane still didn't ring and he was beginning to feel very disappointed. Where was she?

However, after supper, at last she did! 'Hi!' she said. 'Sorry I didn't get back to you earlier but I've been out all day, checking out materials for my jewellery. So how are you?'

His heart leapt when he heard her voice. She sounded as chirpy as ever and thoughts that she might not want to see him were banished. 'Not too bad, thanks,' he replied. 'I'd love to see you.'

'I'm sure you would, darling, but not this evening. I'm just about to put Emma down to sleep and I presume you've got Jonathan with you.'

THE END?

'Yes, I do. He's been keeping me relatively sane while I've been away. How about tomorrow then?'

'Yes, that should work. I'll come over in the afternoon if that's OK with you.'

'Yes, that sounds lovely. I've got so much to tell you. Come round about 3 and bring Emma with you. She can play with Jonathan.' And they said their goodbyes.

David was so excited about the prospect of seeing Jane again that he didn't get much sleep that night, wondering how it would all go. But at least he knew he was still wanted.

The next morning David did a bunch of household chores, knowing full well that it was all just busy work while he waited for Jane. He played with Jonathan as well, who hadn't asked again where his mother was, much to David's relief. They had an early lunch and then he put his son down for his afternoon nap.

And finally the doorbell rang. He rushed to answer it and there she was, his beautiful mistress, holding Emma in her arms. He gave her a peck on the cheek for the benefit of any neighbours who might be watching and then invited her in. He'd already switched the TV to a cartoon channel in the living room and Emma was soon happily engrossed in what was happening on it, chuckling at the antics of the characters. He'd left some of Jonathan's birthday toys on the floor in case she got bored as his son was still sleeping.

Then he and Jane went into the kitchen where he took Jane in his arms and gave her a passionate kiss.

'Whoa! Slow down, big boy!' she said.

'You've no idea how much I've wanted to do that,' he replied.

Then he sat at the breakfast table with her next to him holding his hand as she had when they'd first met, and she said, 'Now tell me all about it.' So he did, hesitantly at first but soon picking up speed and trying to be as honest as he could about his feelings. She listened intently, not interrupting, and when he'd finally come to a shuddering halt, said, 'My poor David,' and gave him a long kiss back. 'So what are you going to do now?' she said after they'd disentangled themselves.

'I honestly don't know,' he said. 'I know I want to go back to work but I don't see how I can with Jonathan unless I get some council help and I haven't asked about that yet.'

She looked at him intently for a moment and then said, 'Strangely enough, I've been thinking about it too and I have a suggestion.' And here she paused.

'Go on,' he said impatiently, his heart in his mouth, wondering if she was going to suggest what he'd thought of as the perfect solution.

'Well,' she said slowly. 'Jonathan needs a mother figure in his life, I'm sure, and I think I'm prepared to be it. After all, I already look after Emma and I don't suppose it will be that much more work to look after Jonathan as well.'

'Are you suggesting we move in together?' he asked, thinking that this was exactly what he'd hoped for.

'Yes, I suppose I am, although for the sake of your neighbours and friends it would just be in a housekeeper's role, at first at least.'

'So let me get this clear. You're actually prepared to move in here with me and Jonathan, are you?'

'Well, you've got more room than I do. I don't think we'd all fit into my little house easily.' And he realised then that she'd thought it all out and was taking charge.

'That's absolutely brilliant!' he said now ecstatically and gave her another kiss, which was interrupted by Jonathan toddling in, rubbing sleep from his eyes. He looked up at Jane and said, reasonably distinctly, 'Where's Emma?' which made both David and Jane laugh. 'She's in the sitting room,' David said and he toddled out again.

'I think they'll look after each other,' Jane said with a grin and David grinned back, feeling that he'd never been so happy, at least not for a very long time. Then she said, 'Can I have a look round the house? I'd like to see where I could work and if there's enough space to put my stuff.'

David realised that she'd never seen most of the house, just the kitchen and the living room probably. He'd bet a million dollars that Jenny had never taken her upstairs. So he gave her the grand tour and she at once fell in love with a smallish box room on the first floor which had a big window in it, saying that it would be perfect as a studio. It was

THE END?

full at the moment of old junk and David said he'd clear it out for her. The house had four bedrooms and one of the smaller ones could easily be done up for Emma, he pointed out. It would still leave space for the bigger spare bedroom, where he'd been sleeping for so long, to be used for guests, if they ever had any. The other small one was Jonathan's.

'It's perfect!' Jane cried when she'd seen the house. 'Can I see the garden too while I'm here?'

'It's a bit of a jungle,' David said. 'I haven't had time to do much with it and, with all this hot weather, everything just keeps growing. But sure.' So he led her back through the kitchen and out into the back garden.

She eyed it critically and said, 'It's got plenty of potential. I'm sure I could do something with it.'

'Better and better. A built-in housekeeper *and* gardener,' David said and she laughed. They went back into the house and continued through to the living room where they found Jonathan and Emma playing a simple game on the floor with the TV still burbling away in the background.

'See?' Jane said, referring to her earlier comment about them looking after each other, and it was David's turn to laugh.

'So when would you like to move in?' he asked now.

'I think we should give it a decent interval, don't you? Maybe a couple of months.'

'I'll go mad without you,' he said.

'No, you won't,' she replied. 'Anyway, it'll give you a chance to get the house sorted and deal with the rest of Jenny's business.'

'Yes, I suppose so,' he said morosely.

'Come on. Cheer up. The time will go really quickly.'

'OK. If you say so.'

'Oh, I do. I'll ring you later,' she promised. But then she had to go and drove off with both kids wailing their displeasure at having their game interrupted.

CHAPTER 21

The next day, Sunday, David made a list of all the things he had to do and the following morning he rang his solicitor first thing.

'Sorry,' he said. 'I forgot to tell you that I was coming back last Friday. So where are we?'

'Good. I'm glad you're back. Could you come into my office soon to sign some papers? As I told you before, the will is very straightforward although you might be interested to know that your wife had an account of her own with a few thousand pounds in it.'

'I didn't know that,' David admitted. 'But it should help to pay off the cost of the funeral.'

'Yes, that's what I thought. But you can't have the money until the will's been probated.'

'Roughly how long do you think that'll take?'

'It shouldn't be more than about six weeks.'

'OK. I'll be able to survive that long. As for coming into your office, I'll do it as soon as I've found a baby sitter for Jonathan.' And after saying goodbye, he hung up with relief. He was pleased he had a professional watching out for his interests.

Then he rang Jane and asked her if she could babysit Jonathan for a bit while he went to his solicitor's. She agreed immediately and they settled on the following afternoon for him to come round and drop his son off. After that he rang his solicitor back and told him of the arrangements and they agreed an appointment time. He sat back in his chair with a feeling of accomplishment. At least he was doing something useful.

Then he thought of starting to clear out the box room and that took him the rest of the morning, leaving all the old junk outside to be taken to the tip while Jonathan hindered him at every turn. But he didn't mind. He looked at the room again when it was empty and agreed with Jane that it would make a nice

THE END?

little studio as there was plenty of light. But it needed a new coat of paint on the walls and the floorboards needed sanding. However, he reckoned he could manage that by himself, thinking that some hard, physical labour was exactly what he needed now.

The rest of the day passed uneventfully except that he disposed of all the junk from the box room at the local tip, taking it all there in the car with Jonathan strapped in and perched on top of an old cardboard box full of rubbish, and Tuesday dawned with him feeling more hopeful now about the next couple of months than he had on Saturday with Jane. First he went to his local B & Q and got himself everything he needed to do the job of redecorating the box room. And then after lunch he took Jonathan round to Jane's but left immediately for his appointment with the solicitor.

He was shown into his office by his secretary and sat in a comfortable chair while the solicitor gathered all the relevant paper work together. He had to sign a number of documents, relating to the house, which had been in his and Jenny's joint names, and the bank, transferring her accounts into his name, before settling back and listening to

Jenny's will. It was a mirror image of his own so he knew what was in it already more or less although Jenny had left a few small things to her parents but David had already taken those up to Scarborough. There were no other bequests, apart from one to Cancer Care, which they'd both had inserted to get their wills made cheaper. As the solicitor said, it was all very straightforward. Jenny hadn't left much behind, he thought sadly, but perhaps it was better that way. After Jonathan had been born, they'd set up a trust fund for him and the final piece of business was related to that. The solicitor asked him if he knew anyone well enough to act as co-signatory on the deeds of the fund, now that Jenny was dead, and David at once said yes. So he was passed a final piece of paper which asked for the signature, address and a few other details of the person assigned as co-signatory and was told he could post it back at his leisure. And finally everything was done and David stood up, shook hands with the solicitor and left after saying his thanks for all the work done on his behalf. 'Don't thank me until you get my bill,' the solicitor joked as he was leaving.

He went straight back to Jane's, told her what he'd accomplished so far, gave her the

THE END?

form to sign before he forgot and drove home with Jonathan after giving Jane a deep kiss. They'd seemed to have come to a mutual agreement not to have sex until she'd moved in with him and he'd more or less come to terms with that.

The next month or so passed quietly with him first taking all Jenny's clothes to a charity shop which he didn't find as distressing as he'd expected and then redecorating the box room and Emma's bedroom, usually while Jonathan was sleeping as he'd learnt the hard way that, if his son was around while he was doing it, he tended to get covered in paint or otherwise manage to get all his clothes very dirty, which made more work for him. He also got rid of his old marriage bed and bought a new one along with a new mattress and new bed linen as he definitely didn't want to sleep with Jane in his old bed and felt much better after he'd done that. He'd taken some more advice from Jane on other improvements to the house too and carried them out, occasionally with the help of outside labour when he couldn't do it himself.

She frequently came round, bringing Emma, and they sat in the kitchen just chatting while the children played. He found out a lot more about Jane and her family during these chats: for example, that she was 35, so quite a bit younger than Jenny had been; she had a sister who lived in Canada with her husband and two lovely children who Jane didn't get to see as often as she would like and her parents were both still alive and living in North London where she grew up. Also that she'd studied Art and Design at college which explained her talent for making jewellery. It was good for David to have this chance to get to know his future 'housekeeper' better and he appreciated her honesty with him about her personal life, although she didn't say much about her 'ex' and David respected this. He reciprocated by answering all her questions about himself as honestly as he could.

Only one other thing of some note to David personally happened towards the end of this period. He got a letter from his solicitor, saying that the will had now been probated and enclosing a fat cheque which was the proceeds from Jenny's estate. It also contained the bill from him and a letter saying, amongst other things, that both he and Jenny had an accidental death policy which would pay out in due course for Jenny. He'd completely forgotten this. The cheque enabled him to pay

THE END?

the solicitor with enough left over to pay off most of his credit card bill, including all the funeral expenses, which had been a worry for him. He knew he was rather old-fashioned in hating to have debts. But perhaps that was the accountant in him speaking, he thought wryly.

∽

But finally the day came when everything was set for Jane to move in. It was a Saturday and she'd already brought much of her stuff round and distributed it where it would best fit. David knew she'd already spoken to Emma about the move and her daughter was very enthusiastic about it. The move itself went very smoothly and, before David knew it, they were all comfortably ensconced as a family.

That first night spent at his home with Jane was probably the most exciting he'd ever experienced. After the children were in bed and asleep, they tiptoed up to the main bedroom, David carrying a celebratory bottle of wine, and undressed each other slowly. Then they just started kissing each other all over and cuddling until neither of them could stand it anymore. David mounted her and proceeded to thrust his penis savagely into her until he came, releasing all the tensions of the past couple of months. But that was just the first of many bouts of passionate lovemaking that night. Jane used all her feminine wiles to make him hard again and again until he finally pleaded for mercy and she climbed off him, obviously sated herself at last.

David turned to her and said with a grin, 'You know this was a new bed, don't you?'

And Jane replied also with a grin, 'Well, it ain't any more, is it?'

'I don't think I can afford to buy a new one every night,' David said, continuing the theme.

'Don't worry. I'll pay for them,' Jane said, before turning over and going to sleep. David looked at his sleeping lover and wondered how on earth he'd managed to land so clearly on his feet but he didn't pursue the thought very far as he was exhausted and quickly fell asleep himself.

He went into work the following Monday with a spring in his step and was gratified by his welcome back. Everybody seemed pleased to see him, especially his boss, and he wondered cynically if this was because

THE END?

of all the extra work he'd created by not being there. But it was good to be back in harness again and he accepted his colleagues' condolences but sidestepped questions about Jenny's actual death. The general consensus seemed to be how well he was looking, with the unspoken 'considering' left unsaid but he just said thanks and left it at that. He certainly wasn't about to tell anybody about Jane. She was his secret.

Time went on with him getting into a routine and Jane seeming to do the same. She'd quickly set up the box room as her studio and spent every minute she could in there, usually when the children were sleeping, making her jewellery. Jonathan seemed to have accepted Jane as a mother substitute, another big relief for David. She had such a different parenting style from Jenny and it was lovely to see him blossoming under her care. He was making rapid progress now in both his speech and coordination although David knew he would always be behind his peers.

But everything was looking good and David himself was happy, an unusual feeling for him.

CHAPTER 22

Jane responds

I was looking through David's photo directory recently, wondering if he had any early pictures of himself in it as there aren't any around the house, and I came across a Word document detailing his and Jenny's life together and then ours. I read it with interest but I'm not going to tell him I did as it's obviously private. But I decided to keep the names he's given us in this extract from my diary anyway out of respect. I might forget to do so in future, however. I had no idea he was much of a writer!

Well, I've gone and done it now, haven't I? What I promised myself ages ago I'd never do again, live with another man! How do I feel about it? Pretty good, actually. I'd forgotten

THE END?

how much fun sex can be and I like David a lot. He seems like a good bloke, even if he is still a little boy at heart. But then I suppose a bit of immaturity won't hurt and, in my experience, it's true of all men.

What do I think about Jenny's death? I was truly shocked when I first heard the news. It was such a waste of a life. But I could see in her, now I look back, the seeds of self-destruction. She was never going to come to terms with Jonathan's condition and I think, in the final analysis, she took her own life because she didn't want to see her son die before she did although, actually, in this day and age there wasn't much chance of that. But I suppose I should confess to secretly feeling a little bit pleased in my heart of hearts that she died when she did, thus leaving the door open for David and myself to get together. Is this terrible? Yes, probably, which is why I will *never* admit it to anybody.

So what are the other good and bad points about living with a man again or, rather, this specific man? Good ones first: To be honest, I like the feeling of security, which, I know, doesn't make me much of a feminist but who cares? I like the fact that he always comes home at the right time and he's always here for the children if needed. I don't think he's going to stray. Also he's a relatively gentle lover and he's never harsh with me, unlike my dreadful ex. At least he's almost always considerate of my needs, which is a big plus. He's a good father to Jonathan, that much is clear, and he obviously loves Emma too. And finally we have similar senses of humour which I think is important.

So now the bad points: I know I've been living alone for quite a while and have got used to my own routine and ways of doing things. But living with somebody always involves compromise and that hasn't been easy. Some of his habits I find irritating but this is a small price to pay. Is that really the only downside I can see to my situation? Well, it's all I can think of at the moment although I'm sure more will rear their ugly heads soon enough.

All in all, I'm pleased with my decision and it will be interesting to see how it works out in the future. The most important thing is that I'm happy and I feel I deserve some happiness at last. One thing, however, I'm quite determined on: I'm never going to get married again. I don't want to feel society's shackles around my ankles and wrists like I

THE END?

did last time and I want the freedom to move out if it all goes pear-shaped. This is why I'm not going to sell my own house but rent it out. Another divorce would just be too much of a hassle. But this is being very negative, I know. I'm not anticipating moving out any time soon.

CHAPTER 23

Not much happened of any note in the next year or so. Jane's parents came round and seemed to approve of David, which Jane was obviously pleased about. David himself was surprised by how forgiving they were of his relationship with their daughter. And Madeleine and Jim came for a couple of brief visits to see how Jonathan was getting on and, after some initial hostility, which Jane managed to defuse successfully, although she admitted to David being very nervous the first time she met them, they agreed with David how useful she was to have around. However, Madeleine did ask him once rather awkwardly if Jane was the cause of the marital breakdown between himself and Jenny, which he most vehemently denied.

THE END?

Also they invited a few of her old friends over for dinner and they both enjoyed that a lot. David found himself liking all her friends and they in return seemed to like him. It was good to have the house full of laughter again. They even managed to go out alone together a few times, either to the cinema, a show or for dinner, Jane having organised a responsible local baby sitter.

But then catastrophe struck from a completely unexpected quarter. David found himself suddenly starting to suffer from insomnia and his muscles started to get stiff and inflexible. He also started to forget things, simple things like the day of the week. Initially Jane put his stiff muscles down to too much love-making and his forgetfulness to, jokingly, early-onset dementia but then she got worried and took him to his GP who referred him straight to the hospital. His GP wouldn't say what her own diagnosis was, not wanting to influence the outcome as she wasn't sure of it herself, she told him.

It took a few weeks for him to get an appointment and when he got there at last, they put him through a large number of tests, including a brain scan. Then, after a couple more weeks for the results to come through, he met a consultant who finally diagnosed him with Parkinson's disease. When he heard this, David protested vigorously, 'But that only happens to old people and I'm not twitching.'

The consultant, however, said, 'I'm sorry, Mr Spiller, but you have many of the classic signs of early Parkinson's. It can happen at any age although it's true it's usually later in life. The twitching, as you call it, sometimes comes later too. But fortunately we have treatments now which can delay more or less indefinitely the more serious symptoms although, unfortunately, we don't yet have a cure.'

'So good and bad news,' David said, half joking. 'But how is this going to affect my life?' he wailed now.

'If you're lucky, hardly at all,' the consultant said.

'Great. Thanks a lot for the reassurance,' David said morosely.

'I'm going to give you a prescription for a drug called Levodopa. It should do a lot to help you with the symptoms. If it doesn't work, we'll try you on something else. There are a few possible side effects but nothing serious.'

'What does it actually do, this drug?'

'It restores your levels of dopamine, which is the main problem with Parkinson's. Come back and see me in a month.'

And David had to be content with that. He left the hospital feeling very depressed and wondering how he was going to break the news to Jane. But, in the event, she took it very well, saying jokingly, 'Well, I guess now I'll have three invalids to take care of.'

He decided not to stop working for as long as possible and continued to go into his job where the symptoms didn't seem to matter as much, although at first he did find the forgetfulness a bit of a problem, but, as long as he wrote everything down, he could cope all right. In the meantime he looked up everything he could find on the internet about Parkinson's disease. It made depressing reading, especially as the consultant was right: there was no cure for it yet. However, the medication he was taking certainly did seem to help quite a lot and he told the consultant this when he next saw him.

'Good. That's what I like to hear,' he said. 'We'll keep you on the same dose then. If you feel there's any rapid deterioration, come in and see me at once although I don't expect there to be as we seem to have caught the problem early enough.'

'Well, I guess that's good news then,' David responded eagerly.

'How are you doing psychologically?' the consultant asked now.

'Not too bad, considering. I have my job and a very loving partner who takes good care of me.'

'Lucky guy,' the consultant said now with a grin. 'If you feel you need any anti-depressants, however, see your GP and they'll sort you out.'

'Thanks, Doctor,' David said and he left after getting another appointment for the following month and feeling better now about the future. When he got home, he told Jane about the conversation with the consultant and she said at once, 'We need to go out and celebrate,' and that same evening after Jane

THE END?

had organised the baby sitter, they did just that, going to one of David's favourite local restaurants and splitting a couple of bottles of decent wine between them.

CHAPTER 24

Jane responds

Poor old David! Yes, it's true. Apparently he has Parkinson's. Even though there aren't any really bad symptoms yet, it must have been an awful blow for him. I've tried to cheer him up as best I can and he hasn't had to resort to anti-depressants – yet, anyway. But still, it's dreadful. At his time of life, especially, and when everything was going so well and he was so happy. How can one family be blighted like this with two fairly unusual medical conditions? It doesn't seem very fair.

Anyway, diary, I have some personal news. I've gone off the pill for the first time in years!! I can just hear the jeers of my friends mocking me, saying, 'What about your promise to never have another child? We thought Emma was

THE END?

enough for you.' Well, I'm allowed to change my mind, aren't I? And anyway who knows if it's going to work? If it doesn't, I won't be too distressed.

Why am I doing it? I think it's got something to do with David's Parkinson's. If he's going to get seriously ill, I want a legacy from him to remember him by in his prime. Also I'm starting to feel a bit broody and know that this is probably my last chance. If it turns out that the baby has Down's, I will most certainly have it terminated this time. I simply couldn't stand the thought of having *another* unhealthy child. But I don't feel that will happen. After all, Emma was a real fluke of nature and nature doesn't believe in two flukes in a row, does it? But of course, if it's healthy, that will, I hope, give me a new lease of life and, possibly, David too. I know it's an awful gamble but it's one I'm prepared to take. So we will see what we will see.

PS I'm still finding it difficult to call myself Jane and my lover David, but it seems to be getting a bit easier now.

CHAPTER 25

Life trundled on for David and Jane. David's symptoms didn't seem to be getting worse, for which he was grateful, although every time he got a twinge in his muscles or forgot something he should have remembered, he was reminded of his own mortality.

And that made him finally decide to make a new will and he went to see his solicitor again. When he told him about his living arrangements, his illness and what he wanted done, the solicitor said, 'Yes, it's a very good idea to make another will now.' So, basically, he left everything he had to Jane, knowing that she'd saved his life by appearing when she had and the will was drawn up and signed.

But then came a bit of *really* startling news. One night when he was just dozing off

THE END?

in bed, Jane came back from the bathroom where he presumed she'd just been washing and said, 'I have something to tell you.'

He half woke up and said, 'OK. Go on then.'

'I think I might be pregnant.'

'What!' he exclaimed, sitting up now. 'Would you mind repeating that?' And she did. 'But that's impossible! I thought you were on the pill.'

'I was but I went off it some time ago, David,' she replied calmly. 'Aren't you happy?'

'It's a bit much to take in all at once, you know.'

'Yes, I suppose it is. I'm sorry to have sprung it on you like this but I didn't want to tell you until I was reasonably sure.'

'It's wonderful news, darling!' David gushed now, enveloping her in his arms. But then he paused and said, 'But what happens if the baby has Down's?'

'I'll have it terminated, of course,' Jane replied, rather brutally to his ears. 'But,' she continued, 'I don't think that's going to happen this time.'

David decided not to pursue her final comment, remembering that, when he'd talked to her about why she'd had Emma and not had her aborted, she'd explained that she was not in a high risk category for Down's and hadn't been offered the test. Apparently it was just very unlucky for her that Emma had the condition. So he left it there and just gave Jane a massive cuddle which she reciprocated.

Later, however, once he'd thought more about the implications of having another baby, he told her, 'You know we'll probably have to move to a bigger house. I don't think there'll really be enough room for five of us here.'

'Let's not worry about that yet,' Jane replied and he knew she was right.

So life went on again with Jane's pregnancy progressing normally and when, at 15 weeks, she had the test for Down's and it came back negative, they were both so relieved they decided to take a holiday, something David hadn't done properly for years, knowing it would be their last chance before the baby came. He had plenty of holiday time accruing

THE END?

to him and with Jane's help he booked a pretty cottage on the internet in the Lake District for a week with plenty of room for the four of them. He also took off the week before the holiday and the week after, giving them three weeks in total.

So, after a first quiet week at home, they set off for the Lake District one Thursday morning, aiming to take it slowly and visit a few places on the way neither of them had ever been to and finally made it to the cottage in the evening. It was as nice as it had looked on the internet and had every mod con imaginable. They were pleased with their choice and went to bed that night really looking forward to the following week.

When they got up the next morning, they opened the curtains and were confronted with a spectacular view of Lake Windermere with the mountains behind. The children were still sleeping, tired after the long journey of the day before, so they went outside into the small back garden and just sat there drinking in the view until Jane got up and went back inside to make coffee. David stretched, feeling totally content, quite sure nothing could ruin this holiday.

And he was right. It was a perfect time for the four of them as the children could play happily in the back garden where it was quite safe. Even the weather smiled on them and it only seemed to rain occasionally at night. One other nice thing was that they were there in the middle of May before the real tourist season started so they didn't have to fight their way through hordes of tourists in the local shops or on the mountains where they went to walk. Jonathan could walk reasonably well by now and Emma was quite strong but they had to stick to the easy paths as they needed to take their double push chair in case the kids got tired. However, as David's own stamina wasn't as good as it used to be, he didn't mind this.

Needless to say, David and Jane spent as much time in bed as they could while they were away, sleeping and romping alternately. And since all the fresh air seemed to tire out the children more quickly than in London, David actually got more sleep than he usually did. So all in all, it was a great holiday and David went back to London feeling better than he'd done for ages. Both he and Jane had got some sun and the children got back with rosy cheeks and a positive glow about them.

THE END?

'We'll have to do that again soon,' David commented after their return.

'Hope you haven't forgotten what's going to happen soon,' Jane replied patting her by-now-quite-large bump and David groaned, for which he got a playful slap from Jane.

Time seemed to fly by now and before he knew it, Jane was in hospital being delivered. The birth was very straightforward, at least compared to Jonathan's, and, when a perfectly normal healthy boy was placed in his arms for the first time, David burst into tears, embarrassing himself considerably in front of the nurses and Jane's mother who was also there. But they were tears of happiness, he knew. They hadn't been told the sex of the baby beforehand, wanting it to be a surprise, but he had been secretly hoping for a boy who he could teach all manner of manly things to, such as how to catch a ball, which he knew he'd never be able to do with Jonathan.

'Hello, Ian,' he finally managed to say to him, using the name Jane and he had decided on if it was a boy. He looked at him, marvelling at the perfect little face which at the moment had its eyes screwed shut and all its dark hair, which he supposed was Jane's legacy although he could have sworn he saw his own likeness in there somewhere. But then the baby let out a lusty cry and he hastily handed it back to Jane who started feeding him. 'He's beautiful!' he murmured and Jane's mother agreed with him.

The baby came home after a couple of days and immediately fitted into the household. David had bought a bassinet which he put next to their bed so Jane wouldn't have to go far to feed him at night. Emma and Jonathan both seemed to adore him although Jonathan, in particular, had to be restrained from treating him too roughly. But he seemed to thrive on all the attention and was soon putting on weight. Jane was determined to breast feed him for as long as possible even though David could see how tired it was making her.

Jane's Mum and Dad stayed with them for a short while in the spare room and David had to admit that they were very helpful to Jane in spite of the fact that they seemed to take over the whole house. So, for example, David was hardly allowed near the kitchen as Jane's mother was permanently in there cooking for the whole family. But, as she was a good cook, David never complained and, anyway, he knew they were only staying a

THE END?

couple of weeks. And after the two weeks were up, Jane's parents did, indeed leave to go back to their own house with promises to be back if they were ever needed. David knew how much Jane had started to depend on her parents but he promised her that he would do all he could to help while he was there and she accepted this at face value. However, it was good to know they weren't too far away.

Madeleine and Jim also came down to see the new baby and to visit Jonathan. But as they stayed in a nearby B & B, not wanting to be a bother in the house, they weren't a problem at all and Jane got on well with them, fortunately, as she had before. And it's true they were very helpful with the children although it took Jonathan a while to remember who they were.

David had decided before the birth to take off the statutory six weeks paternity leave and probably longer and thus was always around at this time. So it was a very full house. The social workers continued to come in fairly regularly to check on Emma and Jonathan and also now Ian as well but, as they didn't stay long each time, they weren't a problem.

After Jenny's death, David had transferred the money Jenny had been getting for Jonathan into his own account, and Jane had a similar amount for Emma. Also he was still getting his full pay so they weren't badly off. Jane also had a small amount coming in for the jewellery she was still managing to sell occasionally. In addition, the accidental death policy for Jenny had at last paid out so David was pleased that money problems seemed to be behind him.

So, in spite of his condition, this was a very happy time for David and he just hoped it would continue.

CHAPTER 26

Jane responds

It's been ages since I had a chance to write an entry in you but I've just been so busy, what with having a new baby to contend with and all. I have, however, been secretly keeping up with David's own memoirs and would now like to add my two cents' worth. Everything he says is true but it's from a man's perspective and I think it may be worth saying something from a woman's.

First, the breast feeding experience: I'd forgotten just how demanding a new-born can be and, while it's true the breast feeding makes me tired, this is mainly just due to the frequency with which I have to deliver milk. Night and day every four hours. But what was even more problematical for me was the pain. If you've ever had a baby suckling you seemingly 24/7, you'll know what I'm talking about. I nearly gave up several times but I persevered and finally got more or less used to it.

Second, sex: I didn't miss doing it straight after the baby came and fortunately David was understanding enough to leave me alone. I think he was probably too scared of losing my affection to force me to do it, especially after Jenny's problems after the birth of Jonathan. It's only in the last week or so that I've felt up to it and we've started again. And now it's with the same kind of urgency we had when we first met, which is exciting.

Third, my parents: I was delighted to have my mum there at the birth even though I was worried in case David felt shut out. But in the event it all seemed to be fine. As for my Dad, I know he was happy for us both. I'm lucky that they're so supportive (and liberal!) and have put no pressure on me to get married again. I can appreciate why David felt excluded from his own house while they were here but am glad he could see how useful they were. It is true, however, that David has been very useful around the house in his own way now that they've left. What about Jenny's

THE END?

parents? I was worried about meeting them that first time as David says but, in the event, it all went off quite smoothly and they don't seem to resent me taking over from Jenny as Jonathan's mother. Which reminds me, one of the milestones in us becoming a proper family was reached when Jonathan started calling me 'Mama' and Emma almost immediately followed suit, calling David 'Daddy'.

Fourth, coping with Jonathan, Emma and the new baby: Quite how I'm going to cope, however, when he goes back to work, I've no idea but I'm sure I'll manage somehow. After all, it's been done before. It is going to happen soon now and I'm grateful to him for taking off more time than he is really owed as unpaid leave even though I know he can now afford it. I know how much he misses his job and his colleagues and can just about understand how important they are to him as a man.

CHAPTER 27

David at last went back to work one month after his statutory paternity leave had ended, escaping from nappy changing and playing with the two older children all day. His colleagues seemed pleased to have him back but ribbed him mercilessly about his fertility and how quickly he'd managed to find a new partner. But he just let it all run over him like water off a duck's back. He was very grateful to his boss for allowing him the extra time off and reckoned that he was lucky she was a woman and could understand the reasons why he'd needed it better than a man would.

He slotted right back into his own office again and worked hard to catch up on everything he'd missed. He did, however, find it quite hard at first to give the work his full concentration as his thoughts were

THE END?

continuously drifting back to his house and wondering how Jane was coping with the three children. But every evening when he returned home, he found the kids being put to bed and was reassured that she must be coping all right. When he asked her about it, she just said, 'What I miss most is not having the time to make my jewellery but I expect that eventually I'll be able to go back to it.'

So things were moving along fine from his perspective until a few months later when he noticed the Parkinson's symptoms starting to get worse again. He at once went to see his consultant who said, 'Relapses are quite common especially as your body gets more and more used to the drug we've been prescribing you. I think it's time to start you on something stronger.' So he gave him a prescription for another kind of medication and David started taking it dutifully.

But this time the side effects were much worse than before and, when David returned to see him yet again, and told him about them, especially his now almost-constant diarrhoea, he was told that this was common and he'd just have to live with it. David groaned and then the consultant asked him whether the Parkinson's symptoms were any better and

David had to admit that they were. 'Don't forget that it's your underlying condition we're treating and, as long as that's being controlled, it's all to the good. If, however, the side effects get much worse, come back and we'll try you on something else. But I don't expect they will. Indeed, I expect you will start to cope with them better and better,' were the consultant's final words to him. So he left the hospital, feeling a bit encouraged but still rather downhearted.

He told Jane all about the conversation with the consultant that night and she commiserated with him and took him to bed. But, for the first time ever, he couldn't get an erection and this depressed him further although Jane just laughed it off, telling him it really wasn't important. But it *was* important, to him at least. However, there was nothing he could do about it so he just turned over and tried to sleep.

In the coming weeks this started happening more and more frequently until David was feeling really desperate and so, reluctantly, he went to his GP and told her about his impotence problem. She was as usual very sympathetic and told him that there could be any number of reasons for it but she gave him a blood test to check his testosterone levels and said she'd get back to him within a few days with the results. David waited impatiently for these and when she called to say that his levels were fine, he was strangely disappointed. He'd been hoping there was some simple medical explanation for his impotence. She did, however, add that she'd do some research into the problem and get back to him again if she had anything interesting to report.

'Perhaps I should just become a monk,' he said gloomily to Jane that night.

'Don't be silly. It happens to all men at some time or another, I'm sure it's only temporary,' she replied but he wasn't so sure and wondered whether there might be some connection with his Parkinson's. His GP hadn't suggested this as a possible explanation so he knew it was probably far-fetched.

But when she rang back the following day to say that there was indeed a connection with Parkinson's, he was pleased in one way that he'd been right in his conjecture and immediately asked her if there was anything that could be done about it.

'I'm afraid you're going to have to go back and see your consultant about it,' she replied. 'I don't know enough to be able to help you.'

David groaned and said, 'Oh, no. Not again. I've already been missing too much time off work because of this blasted condition.'

'I'll write to him and ask him to give you an urgent appointment.'

'Thanks,' David said and hung up, feeling positively depressed now. How dare his body let him down like this! He wondered if he should ring her back and ask her for some anti-depressants but decided to leave that decision on hold for the time being.

But he didn't have to wait more than a week for the appointment letter to arrive and the appointment itself was due just a few days later. He went into the consultant's office after the usual long wait although he knew enough now about how slowly the wheels usually turned in the NHS to always make sure he took a book with him. He started the conversation by saying jokingly, 'Perhaps I should set up a camp bed in your waiting area, Doctor.'

THE END?

'You are welcome to try but I'm afraid you might get thrown out by the cleaners,' the consultant said in the same light-hearted vein. But then he went on turning serious, 'I understand from your GP you have erectile dysfunction. Is that right?'

David had to process the phrase and didn't reply for a second or two. 'Yes, that's right,' he said finally, 'and I'm getting thoroughly fed up with it.'

'Well, the first thing to tell you is that it's very common in Parkinson's sufferers.'

'OK but can you do anything about it?'

'Yes. There are lots of things we can try. But first I need to ask you if you've been feeling unduly depressed recently.'

'I suppose I have, yes, and it seems to have started when I couldn't have regular sex any longer. In fact, I was wondering just the other day if I should go to my GP and get some anti-depressants.'

'The reason I asked is because depression is very commonly the cause of the condition. I propose to give you a prescription for a Viagra look-alike as well as another for some anti-depressants which shouldn't make the problem any worse. The reason I said that is because some anti-depressants unfortunately can do this. As usual come back and see me if there's no improvement. I'll be writing to your GP as usual with the changes in your medication.'

'Thanks, doctor,' he said and he left clutching the prescriptions.

But they did seem to work, remarkably quickly too, and David happily resumed a normal sex life with Jane again, very soon feeling a lot better in himself. 'The miracles of modern medicines, eh?' he said one Saturday night after a prolonged bout of love-making. But Jane didn't reply, just snuggling up closer to him before falling asleep.

CHAPTER 28

Jane responds

With David's enthusiastic permission, I'm making more and more use of the social workers while he's out at work and they're coming in now on an almost daily basis to take Jonathan and Emma to the park. They don't seem to mind and it gives me some time for myself. I try and time their visits so they coincide with Ian's afternoon nap and, as the children like them and I trust them, I don't have a problem with this and so far it seems to be working out well. The older two don't need extended naps these days and they're not out for very long. I refuse to let myself become over-protective like Jenny clearly was. The kids seem to love going on the swings – I think it's something to do with the repetitive motion; it soothes them. So I've been able to start doing my jewellery again, only on a very small scale, it must be admitted, but it's a start. However, quite soon now, we're going to have to start thinking about sending Jonathan and Emma to school and we're quite definitely going to need professional help for that.

What about our sex lives? They're fine at present but, as David says, there was quite a long period when they weren't at all fine. I was also getting depressed by his inability to 'get it up' and, actually, it was me who made him go to his GP in the first place. He really didn't want to discuss something so personal with a woman doctor but I managed to persuade him in the end. I tried to be as reassuring as possible during those difficult weeks but when, in spite of everything I tried to do to help him, nothing worked, I knew he *had* to see a professional. I suspected that a large part of the problem was psychological as I knew how depressed he was getting about his underlying condition. And, in one way, it was good to find out that the problem was common amongst Parkinson's patients. But I am quite worried now about what the future may hold for him. He's still quite a young man after all. But, as with all things medical,

THE END?

there's nothing I can do about it except pray and leave it up to the doctors. And since I'm not even remotely religious, prayers aren't really an option.

CHAPTER 29

Quite a lot of water had passed under the bridge since David's last remarks but nothing of any real interest had happened. He continued to have up and down days with his condition but the drugs, on the whole, were working and even their side-effects were not too bad now like the consultant had suggested they wouldn't be. Jane had a small accident in her car when somebody rear-ended her but she was fine and, luckily, alone. She'd left the kids at home with the baby sitter while she did the shopping. It just meant a lot of hassle with the insurance company to get it repaired but, fortunately, they gave her a courtesy car to drive while hers was off the road.

However, there was now one major change in the household. Emma had recently started at her special school as she was five already,

THE END?

going on six. Jane and David went to visit it beforehand and it seemed like a very supportive environment for a child like her. She loved it and had already, apparently, made a few friends there although she was not very good yet at expressing emotions, and David admitted to himself how lucky they were to have a suitable school not too far away. There she was able to meet other children like her and others too with a wide range of disabilities although he and Jane had been promised she'd have plenty of one-to-one attention.

Apparently, the council was even going to pay for a taxi to take her there and bring her back, which, in these austere times of multiple cuts to budgets, really surprised David. However, the first day Jane took her in her car and she told him later how traumatic it was to wave her daughter goodbye at the door of her new classroom in her uniform of a green pinafore dress. But at least she had the support of other tearful mothers saying goodbye to their children for the first time. Meanwhile David had stayed at home for the morning to look after Ian and comfort Jonathan who had no idea why Emma was leaving him. The concept of having to go to school was still alien to him.

The whole business of getting her into the school and organising the taxi meant, however, filling out millions of forms which was quite a chore and made David wonder how parents with less education than he and Jane coped with the government bureaucracy and got what was owed to them. And, of course, they were going to have to go through the whole laborious procedure again the following year for Jonathan although, hopefully, it should be easier the second time around. But at least the children would be together then.

So that was a big milestone in Emma's young life. She'd been IQ tested already and came out with a score of 60 which David and Jane understood was higher than the norm for children with her condition. Needless to say, Jane was delighted, but not surprised, to hear this. They both knew that Downs was not going to stop her achieving to the best of her ability.

What about Jonathan these days? His motor co-ordination and language were improving quite rapidly, the first probably because of the games he played with Emma and the second because he was interacting now not just with Jane, David and Emma but with others as well, especially the social

THE END?

workers who took him out frequently, and they all encouraged him to speak clearly.

Ian meanwhile was now a chubby little toddler, always getting up to mischief, but with the most delightful cheeky grin which made everybody forgive him anything.

So, all in all, things were on the up for the whole family.

∼

A few months later David came back from work to find Jane wearing a very pretty skirt and blouse he hadn't seen before and an extra special dinner laid out on the table in the dining room with a bottle of expensive-looking wine in the decanter. There were even a couple of candles burning away merrily. 'What's going on, darling? Are the kids in bed already?' he asked as she was obviously bursting with news. 'You're not pregnant again, are you?'

'Don't be silly. Of course not, and yes, they are. I put them to bed early because I have something I want to discuss with you.' And now she hesitated.

'Go on,' he said impatiently.

Jane took a deep breath and then said, 'I left the kids with the babysitter and went into town this afternoon with Alice. Do you remember her?' Indeed he did. She was one of Jane's most flamboyant friends.

'So?' he said.

'I wanted to visit a couple of jeweller's to look at the latest fashions and we were both quite dressed up. I'd put on some of my own jewellery and, as it happened, Alice was also wearing some of mine. The first store we went into I saw a few things that I liked which gave me some ideas but it was in the second that it happened.'

'*What* happened?' he asked now even more impatiently.

'The head buyer of the store happened to be there and he came up to Alice and me and introduced himself saying, "I really like your jewellery. It's quite unusual. Where did you get it if I may ask?" and Alice in her inimitable way replied succinctly, "She made it," pointing at me. I was a bit embarrassed to be publicly outed like this but then he said, "Would you two ladies like to follow me?" And, as he seemed perfectly respectable, we followed him to the back of the store and into a rather plush office where he sat down behind a desk. This is his card,' and Jane now produced a lavishly embossed business card from a pocket of the skirt she was wearing. 'Then, when we were both seated, he asked us to introduce ourselves and Alice did it for herself and me. It was after that he dropped his bombshell.'

'*What* bombshell?' David asked, thoroughly exasperated by all this beating around the bush and not at all sure where she was going with this.

Jane took another deep breath and said, 'He wants to buy my entire production and have the option to buy anything I make in the future. He's willing to pay top dollar if the designs are exclusively his.'

David whistled when he heard this and said, 'That's wonderful, darling. I knew your talents would pay off some day. I understand now why you're so excited.'

'I wonder if you do, darling. It means that I can expand and become a proper business. Of course I'd need capital but, if I have a decent business plan, I see no reason why the bank shouldn't be able to help out.'

'Oh. I see what you mean. Well, I could help you with the business plan but why not? But what about the children? Would you be able to cope with them too?'

'It's going to mean a lot of hard work for a number of years but, if I can't, I was thinking that maybe you could become a house husband. Yes, I know we're not even married but you know what I mean.' And now she looked him straight in the eye and he realised she'd thought it all out.

'I'm not sure if I'm cut out to be a house husband,' he said slowly, 'but let me think about it.'

Jane came up to him and gave him a big kiss on the lips, saying, 'That's all I can ask.'

David knew then he was lost and would never refuse her anything she wanted. 'I didn't know you were so career-minded,' he said.

'I've always wanted my own jewellery business,' she replied simply. 'Now let's eat.' So they sat down and tucked in and everything was as delicious as it looked.

When they'd finished everything, including the wine, David sat back and gave a small

THE END?

discreet burp. 'That was lovely, darling. Now I've had a chance to think it over I don't see why your idea shouldn't work. I could do the accounts for you.' And this comment earned him a long and very sexy cuddle with Jane sitting on his lap. Then they went on up to bed and, after David had taken one of his pills, romped away happily for ages until they both fell asleep exhausted.

CHAPTER 30

Jane responds

I've been so busy that I hadn't had a chance to catch up with David's book or memoir or whatever it is until very recently. But, when I did, I was impressed by the accuracy of his memory. In spite of his condition, he seems to have few problems remembering our conversations almost exactly. Perhaps it's therapeutic for him to write everything down. Anyway, the point is that when I dropped my own bombshell on him, he reacted pretty much as I'd predicted to myself and after a small amount of shilly-shallying, he went along with my plan.

So now I'm in the throes of trying to get a decent business plan together to show the bank. The trouble is it's mostly guesswork but

THE END?

David has assured me most business plans are exactly that. I've decided, if I'm really going to expand, I will need new premises, preferably not too far from home. I certainly won't be able to continue working in my little studio here. I will also need some assistants to help me with the actual manufacturing of the jewellery as I don't want to just sell my designs to the head buyer I met in the store. There will be a much larger profit margin if I can actually sell him the finished products. Also I don't trust him enough not to change the designs. Needless to say, I've been in touch with him several times and have already sent him a sizeable amount of my old, finished jewellery which he has paid me for handsomely. He says he shouldn't have any trouble selling it on to customers. So hopefully, it will be a profitable arrangement all round. And David says that already having a contract with him to sell him my stuff will be a big advantage when it comes to getting a bank loan. Oh yes, I didn't mention that I signed a formal contract with the buyer a few weeks ago now with the aid of a solicitor friend of David's who works closely with him at his company so the whole thing is kosher now.

David hasn't had to stop work yet but he says he is prepared to do so whenever I give the word. There are a few more bits of the jigsaw I need to put in place, the most important being to find suitable premises. I have been looking now for some time and at least know how much, roughly, I will need to pay in rent although I still haven't found anywhere ideal. I have also been back to my old college to visit my teachers there and see if they have any promising students about to graduate who'd be willing to come and work for me and they have come up with a few possibilities. Initially, I'm thinking I'll need two people. And, of course, on top of all this, I've continued to design and make more examples of my own jewellery. So perhaps you can understand now, o diary of mine, why I haven't had time to write in you recently. I'm determined to make a go of this and am getting more excited all the time about the idea. I think even David is starting to get enthusiastic about it.

CHAPTER 31

Having helped Jane with her business plan, David could only wait for the bank to make their decision. However, he was optimistic about the outcome and, when he returned from work one evening to find the baby sitter there and Jane all dolled up, he guessed the decision was in her favour. Jane came up to him and said happily, 'It's all signed, sealed and delivered.'

'Did you get what you asked for?' he asked.

'Very nearly,' she replied. 'At least it's more than enough to make a real start.'

'Brilliant, darling!' he enthused. She'd already found the premises she wanted not far away although, as she'd pointed out to him when they'd visited them, they were not 100% ideal but close enough. And she had her two assistants waiting in the wings to be called. 'So what's the next step?' he asked as they were walking to the local restaurant she'd chosen.

'To sign the contract for the premises and get the equipment moved in,' she replied. 'Then I'll be ready to go in earnest.'

'So when do you think I should stop working?' he asked now.

'Whenever you like, darling, as long as it's in the next few weeks.'

This made him smile and she grinned back. 'OK. I'll hand in my notice tomorrow,' he said. 'Remember I've got to work it off for another four weeks before I can properly retire.' He already knew how much pension he'd get if he retired now and it actually was not an inconsiderable sum - certainly enough to keep body and soul together for quite a while. And, his financial brain ticking over, with the money they were getting from the government for Jonathan and Emma they should be able to get by. But he knew how many start-ups failed in the first twelve months and he was determined this wasn't going to happen to Jane. She'd already agreed to leave him in charge of the money and he knew he'd have to keep a tight hold of the purse strings.

When they arrived at the restaurant, Jane ordered a bottle of champagne. 'I reckon this calls for the boat to be pushed out or whatever the expression is,' she said.

'Fine as long as it doesn't happen every night,' David replied grinning, 'or there won't be much left of your loan.'

'You old skinflint, you,' Jane responded, smiling at him, and he smiled back, happy for her. They had a really good meal and staggered home, giggling like a couple of teenagers.

So the very next day he approached his boss and told her of his decision to quit and why he was doing it now. He could easily have just lied and put it down to his condition but he knew he owed her too much not to be straight with her. She, however, took it very well and said, 'We'll be sorry to lose you, David, but I wish your wife the very best of luck in her new endeavour and you also in your house husbandly duties.' She didn't know he wasn't married and he wasn't about to enlighten her. He didn't owe her *that* much.

'Thank you, Kathleen,' he said simply before returning to his own office to continue work.

The day after that Jane signed the contract for her new premises and swiftly moved in with the help of her two new assistants, both of them girls. David had met them and thought they seemed incredibly young – he could have been their father, he told Jane - but she assured him that they were totally trustworthy and this was an incredibly important attribute if they were going to be manufacturing jewellery for her.

She was using the babysitter a lot at this time until David stopped work, which, to David's way of thinking, was an additional expense. Also she was working very hard now to make a go of the new business so she didn't have as much time for him as either of them really would have liked. But, as she pointed out, this shouldn't last forever and, hopefully, she should be able to start delegating some of the authority to her assistants in the not too distant future.

But then it was time for David to retire and he did so with a heavy heart, knowing how much he was going to miss it. His colleagues

THE END?

threw a big party for him which gave Jane an opportunity to dress up and wear some of her own jewellery. As she said to David, 'If I'm going to be big, I'll need to let as many people as possible see my stuff,' and he agreed. It was actually the first time she'd met most of his colleagues, except for Kathleen, his boss, who'd been to the house twice for dinner and returned the compliment, and one of his best male friends in the office who they'd bumped into once in town. Jane was a bit intimidated by all the testosterone on show at the party but David told her afterwards that this was typical of advertising companies. She did at least make a hit with a few of the wives and secretaries there with her jewellery and gave out her card to them, promising to give them special terms if they bought any of it.

After the party, however, when David had packed up his personal stuff from his office and taken it home, it was time for him to get into a totally different routine. At first it was hard but quite quickly he got to enjoy the children's company, even if it could be a strain at times. He found the manual labouring side of being a house husband very tiring at the beginning – for example, the washing machine and tumble dryer always seemed to be on – and he really appreciated for the first time how hard it must have been for Jane, especially when she was breast-feeding the baby, but, again, once he'd got used to it, it wasn't so bad. But it was definitely strange for him to be in the house without Jane around.

She was almost always out at this time supervising her assistants and buying stock for her enterprise. She'd told David interestingly that one of the best places to get the gemstones she needed was at flea markets. However, she was mostly around at weekends even though she was usually catching up on paperwork then. But she always insisted on being home to read the children their bedtime stories and they seemed happy enough with this arrangement. David was even learning to cook a little, nothing fancy and always from recipe books, but he was proud of himself for doing this.

'Quite a reversal of roles!' he said to Jane once.

'It's been done before,' she pointed out, getting a playful cuff for the remark.

Fortunately, David's health wasn't deteriorating any further and actually he had to admit to being more energetic now

THE END?

than he'd felt for ages. Maybe it was all the physical labour of looking after the children, he thought.

In addition to all this good news, Jane's business was starting to take off much faster than she or David had dared hope. She had so many orders now from the store that she was finding it difficult to keep up the supply and decided she needed to take on another assistant. The two she had already were both working out well, she told him, as they were fast learners, enthusiastic and excited about getting in on the ground floor of a new business. They'd both studied at the same college as Jane had been to herself and thus were well trained. Also they were friends already, another advantage from Jane's point of view.

She got them to put the word out that she was looking for somebody else and several potential candidates came forward. None of them, however, worked out for one reason or another and Jane had to resort to advertising for someone. This time she was swamped with replies and had to spend several days just sifting through all the CV's she received. One of these stood out, as the candidate was young, like the other two, and had only recently graduated from Art school so she was cheaper to employ than somebody with more experience. So she called the young woman in for an interview which went well and she was offered the job, starting immediately. According to Jane, the four of them all got on fine together and she found it useful to have a younger audience on which to try out her designs. Indeed, this was the market she was aiming at: the 20 to 30 year-olds who all now seemed to have some spare cash to spend on looking pretty.

She still wasn't making much of a profit, however, what with having to pay back the original bank loan and all her overheads, in spite of low interest rates, but at least the turnover was looking promising. David knew this because he was doing all her accounts as he'd promised. In addition, the contract with the store was working out well since they had other shops in England which were also clamouring for Jane's jewellery. So, all in all, it was a good first year for the business.

As well as all this, Jonathan had started at school now with Emma, leaving David at home alone with Ian who was growing like a weed now. Jonathan and Emma went together in the same government taxi and David thought

THE END?

they looked very regal sitting up, strapped in at the back. However, Jonathan only went in the morning while Emma now did a full day there until 3.00 pm. They both seemed to enjoy it and, on the few occasions he visited, he wasn't surprised by this as they were clearly getting a vast amount of stimulation there.

So, another turbulent year for the Spiller family, but a good one.

CHAPTER 32

By now David was thoroughly into the swing of his new responsibilities and, in spite of sometimes missing his old job, he was, on the whole, enjoying them. He was hardly noticing his Parkinson's any more. There were crises at home, of course there were, most notably when he managed to scald Ian quite badly in the bath once, but he rushed him off to A & E immediately and they patched him up, looking at David reprovingly all the time. He wondered whether Jane, let alone Ian, would ever forgive him for that but, when he fessed up to her that evening, she took it in her stride, saying simply, 'These things happen.' How different from how Jenny would have reacted, he thought wryly and Jane's reaction just reinforced his love for her. As for Ian, he'd obviously forgotten about it by the next day and was his old self very quickly. The social

THE END?

workers asked him about it the next time they visited and he wondered if the children were all going to be put on the At Risk register but he heard no more about it. Obviously the authorities had decided to treat it as a simple accident.

On another occasion in the middle of winter, the pipes in the kitchen burst and he was left with the most tremendous mess to clear up. It turned out, according to the plumber who he called out, to be an insurance job which was a huge hassle and took him weeks to finally sort out. Meanwhile of course they were left without running water in the kitchen and he began to appreciate how people in the developing world lived. But he managed to cope somehow.

However, probably the most distressing thing for David that happened around this time was getting a letter from Madeleine. In it she said she had been looking through Jenny's laptop trying to find any reason at all why she might have done as she did. And she did find something. She enclosed a few pages of computer printout, purporting to come from 'Jenny's secret diary,' which showed that she had discovered what David had been writing and explaining herself.

When David read in them about her finding out for sure about his affair with Jane at the birthday party and how it had affected her, he was devastated, thinking that he must have had more to do with her death than he'd realised. But then he had another thought: perhaps she'd committed suicide not only because of his affair but also because of her own apparent lack of parenting skills? After all, she'd mentioned that as well in her notes, hadn't she? Perhaps she'd compared herself to Jane and found herself wanting? In which case he didn't need to feel *quite* so guilty, did he? But he still did. He knew, of course, that no answers would be forthcoming and it was probably a combination of factors but this didn't make his guilt go away. Even if he'd been only 50% responsible for her death, it was still terrible.

Madeleine, however, at least did not criticise him in her accompanying letter, just saying that she thought he ought to have the enclosed papers which she had no intention of showing to Jim. But he knew that she had sent him them to make him feel at least a little bit at fault and he couldn't blame her. But he also knew that, for the sake of complete honesty, he had to insert the pages into his own memoir, which he subsequently did.

THE END?

He wrestled with the problem of whether to tell Jane about Madeleine's letter and finally decided he had to. They mustn't keep secrets from one another.

So the evening he received the letter after Jane had returned from work and the kids were all asleep, he tentatively said, 'There's something I need to talk to you about. I got a letter today from Madeleine and it made me feel awful.' And he presented her with the letter.

She read it and then said, 'OK. Are you going to show me the papers she sent you?'

'Yes,' he replied and pulled them from his pocket.

Again she read them but more slowly than she had the letter and when she'd finished, she put them down and said, 'And I suppose you're feeling guilty now about your potential role in her death?'

'Yes, exactly,' he said miserably.

'Well, I don't think you need to. She was a very fragile, unstable person, remember, and probably would have done what she did even without our affair. So, please David, put it behind you, especially as it doesn't affect anything going on in our own lives now. And surely you deserve some happiness at last, don't you?' And with those words she came up to him and gave him a warm kiss.

'Thank you for that, darling,' he said, with relief at the way she'd taken it and pleased too with the fact that she hadn't mentioned the parenting skills issue. It would have been just too much to bear if Jane started to feel guilty herself over Jenny's death. 'I know you're right and I promise I'll try and put it behind me.' And that was the last time the suicide was ever mentioned. With her words Jane really did seem to have exorcised a ghost in David's life, which had been hanging around his neck like an albatross for ever, it seemed to him, He was incredibly grateful for this and their love-making was even more tender that night than usual. And over time he managed to almost forget about Jenny and concentrate entirely on the here and now.

∽

It was about 18 months after Jane started her business and spring had sprung when he broached to Jane something he'd been thinking about for quite a while.

THE END?

'Why don't we get married, darling?' he asked her one evening over dinner. 'You know I love you and I think you love me.'

She looked at him appalled and said angrily, 'Whatever for? Aren't we doing OK as we are?'

He backpedalled and said, 'Yes, of course, darling, but I'm just thinking about the tax breaks we'd get and I'm sure your parents would be pleased.' He knew how, as a business woman now, an appeal to their finances would get her thinking.

'What are the tax breaks then?' she asked now curiously. Here he was on firm ground – it was his field after all – and he started to explain them to her in layman's terms. She listened intently without interrupting and, when he'd finally ground to a halt, said, 'Let me think about it, OK?'

But he persisted, 'What could you possibly have against the idea?'

And now she replied really angrily this time, 'Because I promised myself I'd never get married again after my first husband!'

This took him aback and he retorted, 'You never told me that!'

'There are probably lots of things I haven't told you about myself,' she said, just grumpily now.

He thought he could see a chink in her armour and said placatingly but insistently, 'Will you at least promise you'll think about it?'

'Yes, OK. I'll think about it but now can we please have no more talk about marriage?' And he knew that was the best he could hope for but he hoped he'd got her hooked.

CHAPTER 33

Jane responds

Well, he's gone and done it now, hasn't he? Brought up the dreaded M word. Everything's been ticking along so nicely too. I didn't know he was so keen on getting married and now I'm not at all sure what to do. On the one hand, I can see the advantages tax-wise and he's quite right about my parents – even though they're liberal-minded, they'd be delighted if I 'regularised' my position – but, on the other, I made myself a solemn promise, didn't I? So I'm feeling very torn. I haven't forgotten about my own little house which, since I rented it out, is bringing me in more than enough to pay the mortgage but I know that I'll never return there now. I'm stuck with David and he's right again – I do love him but enough to get married?

However, I'm allowed to change my mind and I think, on balance, I'm going to go ahead with his proposal in spite of my misgivings, although not immediately, and it's not for the reasons he mentioned. Rather, it's for the children's sake. They get on well and I know that in future it will certainly be an advantage for them if we are married. In addition, he told me some time ago that he'd transferred the house into my name in his new will and I'm just too indebted to him to turn him down. So, as usual, we will see what we will see.

As regards the business, he is perfectly correct in his analysis of its situation. However, I'm hoping to start making a small profit by the end of this tax year and that will be the time for celebration – and possibly even marriage? I know how lucky I am to have David doing my accounts as that is one area of the business I'm not at all confident I could cope with. I wouldn't enjoy it, I know that, and at the moment we couldn't afford to get a qualified accountant in.

I have been concentrating more and more on simply the designs for my jewellery and leaving the actual manufacturing up to my assistants. It's good to have a sounding board for the designs and I've found them invaluable

THE END?

for this purpose. And, fortunately, on the whole, they approve of them although I like to think I'm always open to criticism.

I'd now like to address the guilt factor over Jenny's death: I know how hard he took Madeleine's letter and Jenny's comments on the affair but I still think I was right to encourage him to put it all behind him. As for my own potential guilt, having seduced her husband and perhaps being a better parent than Jenny could have been, I do believe that it's perfectly possible I had a greater hand in her suicide even than David but what's done is done. There's nothing anybody can do about it now. But it will always remain a great regret and sorrow for me. And that's my last word on the subject.

One more quick word about David: I really do appreciate him giving up his job to stay at home with the kids. I know how difficult he found it at first but without his support I never would have been able to start my business in the first place. All in all, I'm a very lucky woman!

CHAPTER 34

David didn't mention the idea of getting married again to Jane but one night several weeks later when they were in bed and David was just about to fall asleep, Jane turned to him and said, 'I've given a lot of thought to your marriage proposal and have decided to go ahead with it. So, if you're still willing, let's do it but can we wait a while until the business is a bit more firmly established?'

He woke him up completely when he heard this and he took her in his arms and whispered, 'Of course I'm still willing. That's fantastic, darling, but I hope we won't have to wait for ever.'

'No, but at least until next year, please. By then we should be able to afford a decent honeymoon.'

THE END?

And David realised that, as usual, she'd thought it all out beforehand. So he willingly said he'd wait that long. 'Let's just hope there are no major crises we have to deal with which disrupt our plans,' he added.

'Don't be so negative. What sort of crises are you expecting? Now come here and be quiet,' she said. That shut him up and he just climbed on top of her and made tender love to her.

The next few months rolled by without any 'major crises' and David was becoming more and more optimistic that he would finally be able to call Jane legitimately 'my wife'. And when, finally, the previous year's accounts were all settled and they showed that Jane had indeed made a small but real profit on the business for the first time, she was ecstatic and said one day to him, 'OK. Let's do it.' So David got busy organising everything, from the Registry Office to the reception to the honeymoon. The honeymoon was to take place in San Francisco, a city neither of them had visited but where Jane craftily said she should be able to make some useful contacts for the business. Also it appeared to be a lovely place by all accounts and, while there, they intended to hire a car and see more of California. They would be away for three weeks and asked Jane's parents if they'd be willing to have the children for so long. But they were so pleased that Jane was finally settling down properly they immediately said 'Yes, of course', which had been a major concern for David.

Jane also had to hand over the reins of her company to her three assistants for that length of time but she wasn't too concerned about this. She'd trained them well and they all knew what they had to do. It would probably just mean no more designs while she was away. She had been stockpiling quite a large amount of gemstones for them to work on, all semi-precious as she never dealt in precious ones, and they would be kept busy making up some outstanding orders.

And, finally, the day of the wedding came. Jane's assistants were all bridesmaids and David had asked one of his oldest mates from university to be his best man, one of the very few people he'd managed to keep up with over the years. They hadn't invited many people, only about thirty had been able to accept the invitation with Jane's parents the guests of honour, but they had wanted it to be a small affair anyway. David was only sorry *his* parents couldn't be there to meet Jane. He

THE END?

knew they would have adored her. There was one other notable absence: Jane's sister. She wasn't able to make it over from Canada but she did send them a lovely wedding present and they promised her they'd make it over there for a holiday as soon as they could.

When everybody was assembled in the Registry office that Saturday morning and it came time for Jane to say, 'I do,' she looked at him quizzically for a moment, then grinned and said the words and David thought his heart would burst with pride. He thought she looked stunning in a new, light green gown she'd bought for the occasion. After the formalities were over at the Registry Office where even the children had behaved themselves, probably being a bit intimidated by all the pomp and seriousness, they all went back to the house where they had set up a marquee in the garden, which Jane had somehow found time to tame and now looked gorgeous in the late spring sunshine. They had caterers in who did an excellent job of providing everyone with enough food and drink and even the speeches went off all right, in spite of David's best man making a few rather risqué remarks about his disreputable youth. But at least he didn't mention Jenny and neither did anybody else, which was a relief to David. Meanwhile the kids were all running around getting under everybody's feet but nobody seemed to mind.

Then, finally, everybody left with Jane's parents taking the over-excited children away in their car and David and Jane were alone. Jane said, 'It does feel odd to be in the house when it's so quiet, doesn't it?'

David agreed but added, 'It feels even odder to have finally got you all to myself, Mrs Spiller.' And with those words he picked her up and carried her upstairs to bed.

The next morning they left for the airport and flew off to America. The honeymoon was fantastic for both of them and David didn't begrudge a penny of its cost. Jane even managed to do some business in San Francisco with some samples of her work she'd brought with her and David knew things could only get better for her business now.

They arrived back in London, bronzed, to a showery day and Jane at once rang one of her assistants to find out how everything had gone in her absence, even though she'd been in e-mail contact with them on an almost daily basis, and was reassured that everything

THE END?

she'd asked of them had been completed and was ready to be inspected. Then they picked up the car from the long-term parking lot and drove immediately off home. They had one more night alone away from the kids which they spent quietly, sorting out some of the photos they'd taken of the holiday. But then the jet lag overtook them and they collapsed into bed and slept dreamlessly for ten solid hours.

Jane's parents turned up the following morning with the children and Emma particularly bombarded them with questions about America, most of which they were forced to answer in the negative. Had they gone to Hollywood? No. What about Disney Land? No. Had they met any cowboys? No, again, and so on. But when they showed some of their photos to the assembled family, they were all quite impressed with how much they'd seen, although David wished that Ian was a bit older so he could have appreciated more what his parents had done.

Then it was back into the old routine which Jane seemed to slip seamlessly into although David found it harder at first.

CHAPTER 35

Jane's business continued to thrive. Indeed it seemed to take on a life of its own and she was forced to employ more staff and move into bigger premises, although initially she was reluctant to do this for fear that the whole enterprise would get out of control. But she kept a tight grip on all the management decisions and also the right to veto any of her employees' more unwise moves. Quite soon, however, the company was making a decent profit and she and David woke up one morning to find they were positively wealthy. But it wasn't the money that still motivated Jane. Rather it was the sheer pleasure she got out of designing things which other women wanted to wear.

Meanwhile they had built an extension onto the ground floor of the house at the back

THE END?

with its own bathroom for Ian, rather than buying a new house, and had it decorated to his taste, which delighted him. He felt very grown up having his own private space where he could invite his school friends and make as much noise as he wanted. And, as he was learning the electric guitar now, David also was pleased with this decision.

Ian had, in fact, nearly finished primary school by now and Emma and Jonathan were well into their teenage years with all the problems that implied. But David had been a house husband for so long now that he felt he could cope with anything the children threw at him. They'd even managed to get in a few more holidays, mostly in Britain with the kids, although the two of them had got over to Canada once where they were shown around by Jane's sister, which was a great experience for David. He and Jane were still the best of friends and Jane never mentioned any regrets she might have had about getting married. So everything was basically fine in the Spiller household.

But there, still rumbling away in the background, was David's Parkinson's. There had been no major flare-ups of this for quite a while but David was continually aware of its presence. And one day when he started twitching uncontrollably, he assumed that he would simply be in for many more years of it. He at once returned to the hospital where he saw another consultant, his original one having retired, and was told that, unfortunately, there was not much the doctors could do for him now and he'd just have to live with it. He asked whether surgery was an option but again was told no, owing to the type of Parkinson's he had. So he left feeling very depressed and wondering if he should get another opinion.

Jane was very worried about him too and said that, as money was no longer a problem for them, he could easily go for example to America to get a second opinion if he wanted to. So he did quite a bit of research on the internet and finally found someone much closer to home, in Edinburgh in fact, who seemed to be preeminent in the field. He asked for a private appointment with the man, a Professor Wilkins, and got one very quickly. He decided to fly to Scotland as it was much more convenient than driving or the train where he would have to face the distaste of the other passengers for his condition.

THE END?

So one Friday morning Jane took him to Heathrow as he was no longer safe to drive and they boarded a plane for Edinburgh, using the Special Assistance facility which meant he could get the use of a wheel chair at both ends. They took a taxi when they got there to the hospital where the Professor saw his private patients and waited just a few minutes before being called in.

They found him surrounded by David's notes, which had been forwarded to him by his hospital in London and the list of medications he was on. First, the doctor examined him carefully, asking him lots of questions, some of which were clearly designed to reveal any cognitive impairment, and then he was sent off for an MRI brain scan. The results came back very quickly, within about 30 minutes, and they had a second meeting with the consultant.

This time he looked at David sadly and said, 'I'm afraid you have the early signs of what we call Parkinson's Disease dementia, which is actually quite common in people who've had the condition as long as you. It's related to Alzheimer's and I'm afraid there's no cure for it yet although we're working on some interesting ideas.'

Jane at once asked, 'Is there nothing you can do for him?'

'We can try your husband on some other drugs but I'm sorry to have to tell you that it's a deteriorating condition so I doubt if they will help for long.'

'So what kind of life do I have to look forward to?' David asked, slurring his words slightly as he'd noticed himself doing recently.

'That is a very difficult question. You must try to think positively and not let it get you down although I know that's easy to say and much harder to put into practice.'

'How long then have I got to live?'

'Another very difficult question. Maybe a few years, maybe many years. I'm sorry not to be able to be more optimistic or more specific but I have seen this too often and I'd hate to mislead you.'

'Well, thank you, doctor, for your time,' David said, rising with difficulty to his feet and extending his hand.

The consultant shook it firmly and said, 'I'll be writing to your doctor in London with

THE END?

my recommendations for changes in your drug regime. The very best of luck to you.' And he opened the door for them to leave.

On the way back to the airport David didn't say a word and Jane left him to his thoughts. But then on the plane she said suddenly, 'You know I'll give you all the support you need, don't you?'

'Thank you, darling. I know you will,' David replied briefly before lapsing back into silence again. He knew the twitching, if not the dementia, would prevent him from typing on the computer eventually and decided that this memoir might as well end here.

∽

So thank you, world, for giving me a second chance at life with 'Jane' after 'Jenny's' death and for all the good memories I have stored up although how long they will stay in my memory is anybody's guess. Dementia sounds awful but it happens so gradually that the sufferer is hardly aware of it. If I live a few more years, I'll be grateful. Of course, I might make a miraculous recovery, in which case I'll probably delete this final paragraph and continue this manuscript. But it doesn't look very likely.

So, goodbye all my darling family. Please try and remember me as I was and not as I'm likely to become. If I forget you all in time, forgive me.

The end?

CHAPTER 36

Jane's final response

I haven't written anything about David's story for ages but I've been following it closely and believe that all the facts he has included are true although they are written very much from his own point of view. But now he seems to have stopped his writing, I know I must add something to it.

I recently admitted to him that I'd been reading it from the very beginning and had occasionally added my two cents' worth, written from my viewpoint. But his only reaction was to ask what I thought of it and whether he could include my extracts in it for completion's sake. I told him honestly that I'd enjoyed it and said I'd certainly pass my writing on to him if he really wanted to include it.

I also asked him why he'd changed the names and written it all except the final paragraph in the third person, rather than the first, and he said that it was partly an experiment to see if he could do it and partly because he wanted to depersonalise it, especially at the beginning, and then he just got used to doing it, which I suppose I can understand. As for the final paragraph, he said it was time to admit that everything he'd written was indeed about himself. I asked him no more questions about the manuscript, except to enquire what he wanted to do with it now that it was finished and he told me he didn't care. He'd written it for himself but if I thought other people might be interested in it, I was welcome to publish it in any form I wanted.

<u>Several years later</u>

These last few years have been hard for me but obviously much worse for David. I looked after him for as long as I could at home but, when his dementia got too advanced, I had to put him in a care home. This was one of the most difficult things I've ever had to do as he

THE END?

was very distressed about it. Although I took the children there every day when I could, they were devastated when he no longer recognised them, Jonathan especially, as he couldn't really understand what was happening to his father. However, fortunately perhaps, he died there quickly and painlessly, according to the doctor, one night of a massive heart attack.

I've only now, since his recent death, decided to release this manuscript into the wider world for general scrutiny as I think it's a fine testimony to my late husband. So goodbye now, 'David', as I've got used now to calling you in this, my own diary, whenever I refer to you.

ABOUT THE AUTHOR

After leaving university in London, Richard Sloane roamed the world as a peripatetic English teacher for about twenty years, teaching an enormous variety of students up to and including university level, with just a couple of years back in England to do further studying. Then he returned to live in Cambridge and continued teaching for roughly another twenty years until he was forced to retire for medical reasons. After this he became a full-time author and has so far published seven novels for adults and a number of books for children and young people. These can be viewed on his website at: richardsloanebooks.com and are all available for purchase on Amazon.

CPSIA information can be obtained
at www.ICGtesting.com
Printed in the USA
BVHW032147231019
561779BV00008B/3/P